Deceiving the Earl

KIRSTEN S. BLACKETER

Deceiving the Earl

Copyright © 2018 Kirsten S. Blacketer

Cover Photo: The Midnight Muse

Cover Design: Samantha Holt

Editor: Deadra Krieger

Published by BlackShip

First Print, May 2018

Print ISBN: 9781966905103

Dedication

To Robert Downey Jr and Benedict Cumberbatch, who made me fall in love with Sherlock Holmes.

To Andrew and Mark, who made wish I had gotten the part as Irene Adler. Thanks for the memories.

Table of Contents

Chapter One

London, 1895

Adele approached the townhouse with apprehension stirring in the pit of her stomach. The four story, brick structure loomed over her. Dread settled deep in her mind. Employment in this house would both be a salvation and a curse. She never wanted to resort to such measures, but her situation could not be helped. Adele sought justice for her family, may they rest in peace.

Jameson secured her a position in the house without references. The servants' association with their former employer ensured employment in Lord Dorrington's house. For that, Adele would be forever grateful. The loyal servants who worked for her family for years deserved to have security after such devastation.

After taking a deep breath, she knocked on the servant's entrance. She spent her entire life learning to become a lady, and yet it mattered not one wit. She could never become Miss Adele Prescott again. Her past faded into the distance. Adele's greatest challenge aside from losing her entire family in one fateful blaze lay beyond the carved door before her.

A familiar and welcome face greeted her when the door swung open. Elizabeth stepped aside and allowed her entrance into the house. Her smile glowed with excitement. "Come in, come in." Elizabeth welcomed her. "You must be nervous," she whispered taking Adele's outer garments and depositing them in a small closet next to the door.

Adele inclined her head and offered a hesitant smile. "I

admit to being self-conscious. What if he should recognize me?"

Her friend returned the smile. "Never you mind the master. He is often preoccupied in his study for days on end."

"Does he not venture from the house at all?" Adele asked, curious as to her employer's habits.

"Miss...excuse me, Anne," Elizabeth stumbled over the words. "This may be more difficult than I had anticipated."

Adele agreed. Her attempt to become someone else proved to be a challenge. Six months lying abed recovering from the injuries she sustained in the fire left her much time to become accustomed to her new identity.

"Margaret and Jameson are in the kitchen. Andrew is in the stables. You are to fill the position of the housemaid." Elizabeth rested her hand on the door handle and gave Adele a reassuring smile. "The master believes you are Andrew's sister. I shall teach you all I know. Do not concern yourself. We shall be well cared for here."

With a nod, Adele followed her friend into the kitchen. Margaret stood busy over the stove preparing what looked to be the master's evening meal. Jameson arranged a tray with the necessities of a dinner for one. They both looked up when Adele and Elizabeth entered the room.

"Saints above, dearie, you look quite fine this day. Seems as though those salves I insisted upon helped with the scarring." Margaret wiped her hands on her apron and approached Adele. With a gentle touch, she turned her face and inspected the right side, brushing her fingertips along the puckered flesh tracing her jaw.

Her eyes squeezed shut at the touch. She had yet to see her reflection in a mirror since the fire. The small lodging where they nursed her back to health held none of the conveniences she had been accustomed to growing up. Her mind still reeled from the tedious and painful recovery process. Her scarred face and hands reminded her daily of her family's fate and her current situation.

Margaret tipped Adele's chin up, and she opened her eyes. "Best put on a smile, love. Hard work will chase those horrid memories away. If you need anything, you let me know, or ask Jameson or Elizabeth. We will set you right in no time."

Her matronly smile soothed a bit of the ache stinging Adele's empty heart. She glanced at Jameson who stood watching the entire exchange alongside Elizabeth. They both shared warm expressions in an effort to instill a bit of courage in her soul. No one would expect to see her on the street dressed in a maid's uniform, nor would they expect her to be serving in the house of the man who had brought her family to ruin.

Distrust churned in the pit of her stomach. Oh, the servants believed him to be a fine man. But since he had taken them all on as his personal staff after the horrible incident, it redeemed his character. Adele could not be as forgiving, or as trusting.

She wanted to believe them. However, after dwelling on nothing except his involvement with her father and their scientific partnership, she could only assume he had something to do with her family's deaths.

Adele brushed her hands over her apron. "Shall I begin then?"

Margaret beamed as she resumed her post and ladled soup into the waiting serving dish on the tray held by Jameson.

"Follow me, Anne," Elizabeth said with a small chuckle. Adele followed her up the staircase. "The main floor holds the dining room and the parlor. The second floor is the drawing room and the master's study. While the third floor has two bedrooms, and the attic is where Jameson's room and our bedroom are located."

"We shall be sharing a room then?" Adele asked.

"Of course. It will be like we are sisters." Elizabeth tried to put a positive light on the situation. Bless her for that.

After spending so much time living with Margaret in the small flat, Adele hoped to get to spend some time in a room of her own. Deep inside she chastised herself for being so selfish. She should be glad just to be alive with a roof over her head and not wandering the streets, or heaven forbid, the slums. Adele whispered a prayer of thanks.

They ventured into the study where a tall mechanical cylinder stood in the corner. The gears and mechanisms on it whirred and spun, making a soft hissing noise as it rotated.

Adele stared at it, fascinated by the intricate copper and silver gears as they moved. A chain dangled from the side. When she reached for it, Elizabeth stopped her with a gentle hand.

"It would be wise not to touch this one." Elizabeth eyed the contraption with a wary glance. "Cheeky blighter has bitten me one too many times."

"It bites?" Adele snatched her hand away. Her eyes fixed on the machine, widening as they roamed over the casing. "What does it do?"

"I have not the faintest idea. But every time I dust it, there is an odd sensation that courses through me and burns my fingertips." She backed away from it. "It bites."

Curiosity nipped at her mind. She wanted to know more about this machine, but before she could ask, Adele found herself being drawn toward the exit by Elizabeth's insistent hand.

She noted the picture framed box set into the wall outlining the entrance to the dumbwaiter. It rose through the wall between the dining room and the parlor boasting a door to either side. A small panel of buttons twinkled with lights beside the encasement.

"What an odd little contraption." Adele approached the dumbwaiter.

It beeped at her.

Adele stopped, staring at the panel of lights.

"Oh, never mind Otis." Elizabeth pressed one of the

buttons and the door slid open. The box seemed a reasonable size, perhaps three feet wide, two feet deep and two feet high. Enough to accommodate a large serving tray.

"The dumbwaiter has a name?" Adele asked. While her home possessed its share of modern conveniences, none of them enchanted her as much as these.

Elizabeth gave a small nod. "Yes, he is programmed to deliver the master's tea twice a day, but the bloody machine always seems to arrive at the oddest moments, even when he has not been summoned."

Adele could not stop the smile from springing to her lips. The dread she felt upon arriving at this house melted into a nagging awareness in the back of her mind.

"Mind your fingers, though, Otis has caught mine near half a dozen times. Poor Jameson has quite a story to tell on that account as well." She straightened her cap. "Shall we set to work then? The master's bedchamber should be prepared."

Following Elizabeth, Adele noted the distinct absence of any personal touches to the rooms in the house. While the adornments were quite masculine and beautiful, they lacked any warmth and personality of the man who lived in the house, save the mechanical wonders she had already seen.

"Where is Lord Dorrington this evening?" Adele asked once they reached the landing outside of his bedchamber.

"He should be returning any moment. Most evenings, he takes his dinner in the study." Elizabeth opened the door and busied herself with the fire. "Always prepare a fire for the master every evening. Once in a while he will venture out with Mr. Prescott, but we do try to have the room ready for him before ten every evening."

Mr. Prescott? Owen? Adele's mind raced as she helped Elizabeth. *My cousin.* She had forgotten the two had a friendship that went back to childhood. A sudden wave of fear gave her pause. *What if he recognizes me?* She remembered her cousin being charming and attentive. He seemed to always be aware of his surroundings, but never quite to the point where he would acknowledge a servant other than to summon another dram of whisky.

"Does Mr. Prescott often call upon Lord Dorrington?" Adele feigned an air of idle curiosity.

"Aye, he does, although I have rarely set eyes on him in the six months I have worked in this house." Elizabeth turned down the blankets on the bed, gesturing for Adele to help her. "Jameson always escorts him to the study and to the door. He only ever calls in the evenings when he wishes for company to the club."

Adele nodded, her fingers smoothing over the rich fabrics lining his bed. It had been too long since she felt such fine linens, let alone slept on them. All the things she had taken for granted became a vague memory, a longing for her innocent childhood.

At nineteen, Adele knew only of life in her father's home. She would have come out in spring had the tragedy not befallen her family. She wiped a tear from her eye and focused on the tasks set before her. Elizabeth proved a patient teacher, even with Adele's inability to focus.

"Anne." Elizabeth's voice shook her from the chaotic thoughts swirling in her mind. "Would you please draw the curtains closed?"

Adele did as her friend requested and continued to follow instructions, forcing herself to live in the moment, not in the past. She pressed her hand on her heart where the pendant her father had given her rested against her skin, warm and comforting. She took a deep breath.

"For you, Papa." Adele sighed. "I vow he will answer for what happened to you."

Christopher lounged in the wingback chair positioned by the fireplace. He rotated the glass in his hand, allowing the amber liquid to swirl beneath his touch. The fire reflected in the whisky, echoing the darker bent of his thoughts. How he wished the fire would consume him as well.

He shifted the glass to his lips and allowed the liquor to burn a path to his gut. It numbed him, but he needed something stronger and more potent to steal away the guilt and the haunting memories. Perhaps a trip to the Floating Den would give him the reprieve he so desired. Since Owen introduced him to the sweet bliss of opium, he found he craved it more with every passing day. Or rather, he craved the oblivion it created in his mind. A mind that no longer contained his own thoughts and desires alone.

With a tip of the glass, he emptied the contents, letting it settle heavy in the pit of his stomach. He regarded the large gaudy grandfather clock in the corner of his study. Seven o'clock.

The soft knock ceased to surprise him.

"You may enter, Jameson," he called out, rising from his chair.

He moved across the room toward the desk where Jameson placed the tray with his supper. The savory aroma of roasted beef and gravy mingled with the delicate notes of yeast and sugar from the warm, fresh bread. His stomach growled at the sight of the meal.

"You could have Otis deliver this and saved yourself the trip." Christopher turned his attention to the butler.

Jameson's lips thinned when he glanced at the dumbwaiter. "I would rather ensure your meal be delivered on time," he said and then continued, "and without mishap, my lord." He offered a small bow.

As if on cue, Otis' door slid open with a loud ding followed by a series of chirps.

Jameson cradled his hand, Christopher noted. Those two formed quite a distaste for each other over the past few months. Since Otis' mistake nearly cost him several fingers, Jameson avoided the dumbwaiter if at all possible.

Christopher gestured to Otis with his gloved hand. "I

shall see if I cannot adjust his timing gears."

Jameson said nothing, but his eyes shifted away from the wall housing Otis. "As you wish, my lord." He hesitated for a moment. "The new maid has arrived, my lord. She will begin her duties in the morning."

"Ah, yes. What is her name again, Jameson?" Christopher inquired.

"Anne, my lord. She is Andrew, the stable boy's, sister."

"Very well. Please ensure she is apprised of her duties in full measure. I shall not take pity on her if she cannot perform to my standard." Deep inside, Christopher knew he would. How else could he account for this attack of conscience and the sudden acquisition of a full house of servants without references? He shook the nagging voice from the back of his mind.

"Will there be anything else this evening, my lord?" Jameson stood at attention waiting to be dismissed.

Christopher sat at his desk and removed his gloves. "That will be all."

With a brusque bow, the butler left him to his supper.

He gingerly picked up the fork with his left hand. The metal of his prosthetic hand grated against the silver. He sighed. Perhaps he should eat with the gloves on. He disliked wearing them all day, but it seemed to be the only way to avoid any contact, however accidental. The consequences of such an encounter would be most unpleasant.

The roast melted on his tongue. He savored the flavors and ignored the inconvenience caused by his infirmity. Blasted war. He regretted many things, including joining the military. Charging off and embroiling himself in a foreign conflict had cost him his left hand. Thankfully, he knew a coppersmith who helped him design a suitable and stylish replacement appendage. Although, after the incident in his laboratory, he found the gloves protected both his deficiencies from the public eye.

After a few more bites, the flavor of the meat and gravy

turned to dust on his tongue. His hunger sated, he pushed the plate away. The memories stole his appetite once again. Nothing stole his passion for living so much as the constant reminders of the past. No matter how much he attempted to atone for his sins. There would never be atonement.

He pushed the tray away and leaned back in his chair. Christopher tugged the gloves on and steepled his fingertips in thought. The flicker of the flames caught his attention once more. If only he could find a way to regain control of his life, of his mind, then he could learn to live again. But he would never be able to forgive himself.

Another knock disturbed his solitude.

Jameson entered the room. "Mr. Prescott to see you, my lord." He stepped to the side.

"Dorrington, old chap, why in the devil are you shut up in the house?" Wearing a lopsided grin, Owen sauntered into the room. Everything from his side-swept blond hair to his tailored suit presented Owen in the most flattering light. He stepped up to the decanter and poured himself a dram of whisky. When he turned toward Christopher, his blue eyes glimmered in the dim room. He sipped the drink and leaned against the table.

"Well, then, shall we venture to the club?" Owen watched him with measured curiosity. "Or perhaps off to the Floating Den to chase the dragon? What mischief shall we conjure up this evening?"

"Since when are you not mischievous?" Christopher asked. "You seem to forget how long we have known each other."

"Ah, that may be true, but you cannot know all my faults, can you?" Owen downed the whisky. "Come then, let us go paint the town."

Christopher sank into the chair beside the fire once more, his gaze lost in the flames. "I fear I am not one for entertainment this evening."

Owen sat in the chair opposite him. "It has been six

months. Surely you cannot still be blaming yourself for what happened." He offered a sincere but sad smile. "Fires are always a hazard. They happen every day. No one is to blame. You must not torture yourself with all this guilt."

"Had I not brought that damned metal back from Khartoum..." He allowed his voice to drift off, alluding to the consequences of his actions.

"You think your experiments caused the fire?" Owen asked.

"I know nothing for certain." Christopher clenched his hand into a fist. *Except that I shall never be the same man I once was thanks to that blasted shard of metal.* He spoke the words to himself, afraid of speaking them aloud. No one knew the truth of that failed experiment, except his partner, who died in that fire along with his family.

"I see the new servants have worked out well for you." Owen redirected the conversation to a less painful topic and stood to pour himself another glass. "You took on all of my uncle's displaced servants then?"

"Not all of them. But I did help them all find suitable positions after the fire." He tried at least. Some of them disappeared, lost to the fire, he gathered.

"Damned decent of you. And taking up residence in town instead of hiding away in the country will do you good."

Christopher wanted to shrug, but he refused to react. Truth be told, he hated town. He hated having to be part of society. But since he inherited his brother's title, he was required to make an effort. A second son no longer, but an heir. The word curdled on his tongue every time it came to mind.

"Perhaps if you returned to your scientific pursuits, you could put an end to all these feelings of guilt. Find your spark again." Owen tipped another drink back after a hearty salute. "Tinkering in the laboratory always seemed to bring your spirits 'round."

"There is nothing for me there." Melancholy settled around his heart.

Owen sighed in defeat. "At least come with me to the club this evening for an hour or so." Concern etched his normally charmed features. "A night out will serve you well."

Christopher could no longer deny his friend's persuasive request. "Only for an hour."

As he readied to leave, Christopher pondered his friend's words. It was true. Fires happened every day. Could he truly blame himself for an accident?

While the fire might not have been of his doing, he contributed to the events leading up to that fateful night. There were still too many unanswered questions. Someone wanted the metal fragment he had been studying. They wanted it bad enough they were willing to sack the laboratory and destroy months of research in the process.

Hiding that damned piece of metal had been the wisest course of action short of destroying it. He wished his partner told him where in the devil he hid it before he died.

Chapter Two

The first evening spent as a servant presented complicated emotions. Adele adored Elizabeth and found she had no qualms in sharing a room with her. The manual labor kept her mind as well as her hands occupied. Lying awake in the dark hours of the morning, the loneliness of reality sank deep into her soul. She missed her family and her friends. No one in the world, except for the servants who saved her, knew who she truly was.

When dawn broke and Elizabeth roused her, the thankful reprieve of work rescued her from her isolated, morose thoughts. Adele learned her place and the tasks required of her. Elizabeth and Margaret instructed her in every duty to ensure she became a reliable and believable maid. Even with all her instruction, she could not shed her upbringing as a lady. It followed her like a shadow tainting every action she took, every word she spoke.

Adele dusted the shelves in the study, gently removing the ornaments and books, cleaning each one, and replacing them. Elizabeth swept the ashes from the fireplace and set to cleaning the grate. She hummed as she worked, and Adele found herself drawn into the infectious melody.

Having dusted the entire room, Adele approached the copper cylinder in the corner. Hesitation and curiosity mingled in her actions as she approached the contraption. A gentle hum reached her ears.

"What did you say the purpose of this...machine is?" Adele asked.

"Lord Dorrington says it produces energy current. Whatever that may be." She wrinkled her nose in a distasteful manner. "All I know is it bloody hurts when you touch it."

"So, shall I attempt not to touch it then?" Adele circled

the edge of it. Part of her wanted to feel the bite, as Elizabeth put it.

The gears and mechanisms whirred inside the wall and popped with a ding as Otis' door slid open.

Adele gasped at the sudden intrusion. "Otis," she murmured under her breath as she approached the dumbwaiter. When she glanced inside, the box stood empty.

"Again, Otis. Really, this nonsense must stop." Elizabeth came alongside Adele and shook her head. "The master should fix your timer."

"He does this often?" Adele pressed her hand to the panel of buttons. Otis beeped and his door slid closed again.

"Nearly every day." Elizabeth wiped her hands on her apron. "It irritates Jameson something foul."

"Doesn't everything irritate Jameson?" Adele said with a chuckle.

"Excellent point," her friend said with a smile.

"Being on this side of things certainly gives me a proper respect for the work you all do every day." Adele spoke in a quiet voice.

"Just keep up with us, or you will be out on your backside."

The sound of the door opening interrupted their solitary moment. A wave of fear forced Adele to spin around, turning her back to the door. She would not want to be caught idle while she was supposed to be working.

"My lord," Elizabeth said behind her. "Pardon us."

"Ah, yes, I forgot you would be here at this hour." His voice tugged at her memories. While familiar, it echoed strange in her mind, as though distant, foreboding, and strangely alluring.

Adele turned, keeping her head down. She bobbed a small curtsy and avoided meeting his gaze.

"Is this the new maid?" he asked.

"Aye, my lord, this is Anne." Elizabeth stepped to the side as he approached them.

He paused before Adele. She studied his pressed trousers and the tips of his polished shoes.

"If you will beg my pardon, my lord, I shall fetch some coal for the fire." Elizabeth's voice echoed from the doorway.

"Very well," he said in dismissal.

Adele stood as still as her trembling body would allow. Her heart pounded. There would be no way to hide herself from him now. Most masters were satisfied when the work was completed and their servants remained silent. Adele closed her eyes and took a deep breath. *What if he recognizes me?*

"Anne." Her alias on his lips sounded almost like a challenge.

"Yes, my lord," she replied, her voice steady, unlike the emotions boiling beneath her calm exterior.

"Will you not meet my eyes?" he asked. When she hesitated, he tipped her chin up with his gloved fingertip.

With a deep breath, Adele met his gaze. She faltered for half a second, not because of his familiar face, but because of the shock of his deep, soulful hazel eyes. Never in her father's long acquaintance with him, had she taken the opportunity to converse with him, let alone share a lingering look.

Lord Dorrington was even more handsome than she remembered. His dark hair lay in waves, longer than fashionable, but neatly kept. The strong lines of his jaw were shadowed by a days' worth of stubble. It lent him a roguish air. Her breath caught. From his dark, penetrating gaze to the soft smile haunting his lips, Adele found herself mystified by the man before her.

He only ever visited her father to work in the laboratory. Everyone knew him to be a reserved sort, especially after he returned from the war and inherited his brother's estate. Adele wanted to despise him for the path he led her father down. But seeing him, eye to eye, she saw the despair behind the gentleman's façade.

His fingertips brushed along her scar. "An injury from

the fire, I presume?"

"Yes, my lord." Adele suppressed the sudden desire to run as he inspected her face.

"You were fortunate to escape with your life, my dear." He nodded before dropping his hand. "How do you find your new post?"

"Very well, I thank you, my lord." Adele tried to keep her answers direct and simple.

He tilted his head and regarded her with a keen eye. "Have we met before? Upon my visits to your former employer's estate perhaps?"

"It is possible, my lord. However, I do not recall." She bowed her head, unable to bear the constant scrutiny. Surely, he remembered her.

"I shall leave you to your duties then, Anne." He turned to leave before pausing in the doorway and gesturing to the cylinder in the corner of the room. "Oh, and careful as you dust the inverter. It is liable to produce an electric shock that may be uncomfortable."

With those cryptic words, Lord Dorrington left her.

Adele collapsed in a chair and pressed her hands to her cheeks. Relief flooded her as she realized he did not recognize her. The dye in her hair and the scarring from the fire must have altered her enough to allay any suspicions he might have. She allowed a smile to cross her lips. Her ruse would work. He could not hide the truth from her. She would have the truth of what Lord Dorrington had convinced her father to study that cost them all so much suffering.

After dinner, Christopher sat in his study leafing through a stack of notes he made during his experiments with the mysterious metal. The fate of that damned fragment haunted him, just like his encounter with the new maid that afternoon. He picked up the glass of whisky and sipped as he scanned the narrow handwriting. He pushed the notes aside and closed the folio, hiding them from view.

"Damn and blast," he muttered as he drained the rest of the liquor. Christopher rubbed the bridge of his nose and the crease between his eyes. The aching in his head and the intemperate nagging of his guilty conscience made him long for something stronger. He glanced at the clock. Half past nine. He could visit the Floating Den and return before the effects pulled him under.

He admitted a mild curiosity when it came to the new housemaid. However, meeting her proved far more unnerving than he anticipated. Was it not for her dark hair, her haunted eyes, and the scarring on her delicate pale jaw inching like tendrils onto her face, he would have thought Alastair Prescott's daughter returned from beyond the grave to haunt him.

In all the years he worked alongside Alastair, he never took the opportunity to socialize with his family. Although he saw his partners' daughter, Adele, in passing a few times, there had never been occasion to speak to her. She always seemed ethereal, like a specter floating in the distance.

What could he say to a girl of seventeen whom he had no inclination toward? Never mind Christopher always seemed awkward when it came to society functions and social etiquette. Being thrust into a position of status and responsibility crushed his dreams of studying science and tinkering in his laboratory. After the fire, he walked away from his passion knowing that the only thing it led to would be more death and destruction. He was not willing to hazard the future consequences of his experiments after what happened.

He shoved the chair back and stood, heading straight for the decanter sitting on a table by the window. After pouring a healthy dram, he jammed the stopper back in. The decanter wobbled with the force and he steadied it with one hand, cradling the glass in the other. Perhaps he would call Jameson to fetch his coat and hat. The spring rain continued outside if the streaks on the windowpane were any indication. The Floating Den always docked at Westminster Pier at ten, then Hyde Park at eleven. That would give him all the time he needed.

He drained the glass and pushed it aside, his determination set. Upon crossing the room, he unhinged a cap on the copper pipe next to the door and pressed the number one on the keypad next to the opening. A few seconds later, a voice echoed through the tube.

"You rang, my lord?" Jameson asked.

"Yes, Jameson, would you please fetch my coat and hat and meet me by the front door? I am going out."

"As you wish, my lord." The pipe fell silent.

Christopher flipped the top down and exited the room. Bell pulls seemed so old fashioned. He rather preferred his little contraption that allowed him to converse with his servants wherever they may be in the house. He had them installed when he purchased the house, and they proved useful both for himself and his staff.

He descended the stairs and nodded to Jameson who stood waiting by the front door holding his long coat and hat.

"That will be all, Jameson. Good evening." He donned the outer garments.

"Good evening, my lord," Jameson replied with a small bow.

As Christopher stepped from the house, he stopped short and the door clicked shut behind him. Owen Prescott stood on the steps before him.

"I wanted to see if you wanted to pop over to the club for a round of cards." Owen's friendly smile and easy demeanor often made him feel like a dour old man.

"I was just about to head in the direction of the pier, if you would care to join me." Christopher nodded in the direction of the Thames.

"Sounds like a quality idea." Owen tipped his hat into

place and retreated off the steps as Christopher descended.

The two men fell into step beside one another and continued down Hamilton to Piccadilly.

Owen glanced at his pocket watch. "We should hail a hansom if we want to make the ten o'clock stop at the pier."

Once they reached Piccadilly, they hailed a cab and climbed in. A calm silence descended upon them.

"Something ailing you? You look a bit somber." His friend pulled a cigar from his pocket and lit it.

Christopher exhaled. He had been lost in thought all day and even more so since his little conversation with Anne. He wished he could get inside her mind. Christopher shook his head—no, he did not want that. But everything from her bearing to the way she looked at him with fear and confusion lurking in her blue eyes made him uneasy. And damned if he knew why.

"Your entire family is fair haired, are they not?" he asked.

"My father and I are both blond. Even my uncle and both his children were golden haired. Mother always said it came from our German great-grandfather." Owen looked at him. "Why do you ask?"

Christopher shook his head. "I was trying to remember what your cousin, Miss Prescott, looked like."

"Adele?" He cocked his head in amusement. "Why in the devil are you thinking about Adele? May she rest in peace."

"A random memory came to me today when I was pondering my time at the laboratory," Christopher lied.

"Is that so?" Owen leaned forward in interest. "Are you considering taking up your experiments again?" He nudged Christopher with his elbow. "It would do you a world of good, you know."

"I have not decided anything," He replied with an exasperated look. "But there are details, answers I must have if I am to put my soul to rest."

"Six months have passed, my friend," Owen said. "You

must move on with your life. Take up another hobby. Attend some events. Rejoin society and find a suitable wife, for heaven's sake. Like me."

Christopher's gaze snapped to his friend. "Like you? What foolishness are you on about?"

The carriage rattled around them drowning out their conversation to anyone but them. "There is the loveliest flower, the daughter of the Duke of Coventry, a rare blossom indeed, which I intend to pick for my very own." He winked.

"The daughter of the Duke of Coventry?" He stared at his friend. "And is she aware of your intentions?"

"Not all of my intentions," Owen said with an impish smile. "Would you have me play my hand so soon?"

"Never." He turned his attention back to the road and thought for a long moment. "Do you believe your charm to be powerful enough to sway His Grace enough to grant you his daughter's hand in marriage?"

"While my charm is quite potent, I would never presume to rely solely on it to obtain a fair jewel such as my lovely Viola." Owen took a long drag from his cigar before exhaling the smoke in a mystical plume. "My father's newly acquired rank in society has garnered him quite a bit of attention among the peerage. He has hosted a few events that attracted several of the His Grace's closest friends. While I mourn for my uncle, aunt, and dear cousins, their untimely deaths have paved the way for my father to assert his influence."

The implications of Owen's statement cast an unfavorable light upon Lord Longmont. Such thoughts Christopher did not wish to ponder, especially in the morose mood he seemed to be embracing at the moment.

"You should find yourself a woman at the very least," Owen jested as the carriage rolled to a stop at the pier. "A long night with a favorable woman might be just the distraction you need."

Christopher glanced at his watch. Five minutes until ten. He caught sight of the Floating Den hovering over the water next to the pier.

"I have no intention of purchasing a woman for sexual favors," Christopher replied in hushed tones. They walked toward the pier together.

"A good fuck would set you right as rain," Owen said again as they approached the gangplank.

"In an hour, I shall be perfectly fine."

Owen shook his head and handed both their admission fees to the gentleman at the entrance to the Floating Den. "Perhaps I introduced you to the wrong vice."

Christopher wondered if Owen ever viewed anything in a serious manner. His entire life seemed to revolve around pleasure and a life of ease.

He envied his friend for the blissful ignorance that surrounded him. A shroud of dread seemed to follow Christopher wherever he went. And only sweet opium dulled the constant press of his failures against the cursed heart that beat in his chest.

Chapter Three

The neat rows of books lining the shelves on the far wall called to her. Adele shook the impulse to answer their seductive invitation and instead focused on her task. She lifted the decanter and set it aside. As she polished the wooden surface, her gaze drifted to the floor-to-ceiling bookcase behind the imposing mahogany desk.

The study held a comforting scent. A mixture of leather and books and tobacco. Her father's study smelled very similar to this one, only the masculine aroma beneath it in this case stirred an unfamiliar sensation in the pit of her stomach.

With an inaudible sigh, she replaced the decanter. The desire to read filled her. A wicked part of her longed to pluck a book from the shelf and tuck it into her apron pocket to read by lantern light after Elizabeth fell asleep. It had been six months since she read something aside from the newspaper. Adele longed for the thrill of a novel. Even a penny dreadful would suffice. Books had always been her escape, her world. The life of a servant afforded her no literary luxury.

She turned her attention to the desk and polished the surface, stacking items out of the way and replacing them as she cleaned. By accident, Adele tipped a folio off the desk and onto the floor. She gathered the papers and tucked them back inside. The words caught her attention, but the script made her pause.

Her father's handwriting intermingled with another unfamiliar script. A tear slipped, running down along her cheek. She wiped it off the paper and tucked away what she realized were the lab notes from her father's experiments. After polishing the desk, she replaced the folio as well as the other items she moved and faced the bookshelf.

A torrent of emotion welled in her chest. She missed her family to the point of physical ache. The true pain came from knowing they were not still part of this world and she existed alone. Adele forced her composure and focused on the titles of the books as she wiped the bookshelf. *Verne, Poe, Bronte, Shelley, Chaucer.* Her fingertips traced over the spines. He would never notice if she borrowed one of his novels. Would he?

Wicked and rebellious, her conscience warred in the back of her mind. Her intent should be to keep out of sight and out of mind, but the allure of an enthralling tale bewitched her. Adele slipped *Wuthering Heights* from the shelf and into her pocket before resuming her work.

The soft murmur of voices from the neighboring drawing room startled her. She finished the shelves and crept over to the adjoining door with the intent of closing it when the familiar cadence of Uncle Magnus' voice reached her. She froze.

He, of all people in the city of London, would be sure to recognize her. She hid from view, peeking through the crack between the sliding pocket doors.

"I trust you are enjoying your new status, Lord Longmont?" Lord Dorrington offered his guest a glass of brandy.

"I am," her uncle replied, taking the drink in hand and inhaling the aroma. "It seems quite natural I should take my place as soon as possible. No reason to languish in grief."

Adele bristled at his words. Had he no heart? Did he not care about his own flesh and blood that he would cast aside his mourning to claim his brother's title with little more than a few lamentations and a forced tear or two? Taking a deep breath, she calmed herself enough to focus on their conversation. Revealing herself would cause her identity to come to light. She could not have that.

"Owen tells me you have been working on a contract with the military to develop a new type of ship, a dreadnaught." Lord Dorrington sat across from his guest, facing the door where Adele hid herself. His attention remained focused on her uncle.

"Indeed, I have been in several meetings discussing the possibilities for constructing a new fleet of war ships made from a lighter, more durable metal." Her uncle paused to drink before continuing. "I make no secret of the fact that I am in need of your help in this matter. The metal you and my brother had been working with could have been a viable candidate for this proposal."

"It was a scrap of metal I found while serving in Her Majesty's army," Lord Dorrington said in measured tones as if they discussed this very thing before. "Even if we discovered a viable use for it, there is no reference to determine where it could be mined and collected for a project as massive as what you are proposing."

"There are ways to discover such trivialities," her uncle said with a wave of his hand. "You must be anxious to continue your work with the metal in a laboratory."

"Unfortunately, it was lost in the fire." Lord Dorrington shrugged before draining his glass. "Alistair hid it away after the laboratory was destroyed by thieves."

Uncle Magnus hung his head for a moment. "That is regrettable. But even so, you must have notes on the experiments you already performed."

"My notes were also destroyed in the fire," Lord Dorrington responded with a serious expression.

Adele shifted, shocked at his blatant lie to her uncle. She herself just discovered the folio containing her father's notes. Why would he lie to Magnus? Her hip bumped the door causing it to rattle on the hinge. Lord Dorrington's gaze snapped up to meet hers through the crack in the door. Every fiber of her being wanted to run. Their eyes locked for a half moment before he shifted his attention back to her uncle.

"Ah, well, that is quite a disappointment as well." Her uncle set his glass down and stood. "I do hope you will keep me apprised should you remember anything that may be of use to us in the future. There is a lucrative market for inventions of your caliber that could aid in the protection of England."

"I thank you for the honor of paying me this visit, Lord Longmont," Lord Dorrington said with forced cordiality. "And I am humbled you think so highly of my work. Shall I ring for Jameson to escort you to the door?"

"I doubt that will be necessary. I assure you I am quite capable of finding my way out." Her uncle tipped his hat as they reached the door.

"Allow me to escort you myself." Lord Dorrington cast a glance at Adele as he led her uncle from the room.

Adele knew if she did not make herself scarce in the scant few moments it took him to show Magnus the door, she would be cornered when he returned. Of course he would chastise her for eavesdropping on a private conversation. Fear gripped her. Without hesitation, she scrambled for her cleaning supplies and made her way down the back staircase to the kitchen. He would not seek her out, would he? She knew beyond a doubt he would pull her aside at some point and address her behavior.

The book in her apron pocket hung heavy against her skirts. Guilt enveloped her.

Stupid. How stupid can I possibly be? Taking one of his books, eavesdropping on his private conversation. Adele berated herself all the way to the kitchen.

Margaret glanced up from her cooking. "Hello, love. Have you finished in the study then?"

"I have," Adele replied trying to keep her voice measured and calm. "Would you like me to help Elizabeth prepare the master's chamber this evening?"

"I have already done it," Elizabeth said as she entered the room with her bucket of coal. "Took you long enough to clean the study. Did you stop to read a book?" her friend teased.

Warmth stole along Adele's cheeks and the weight of the

book hung like a loadstone against her skirts.

"Stop teasing the poor girl," Margaret said with a chuckle. "She is not used to this work. But give her time. I am positive she will be running circles around you lot before the month is out."

Elizabeth stuck out her tongue before offering to help Margaret with the cleaning.

Adele busied herself with scrubbing the pots left from dinner. She hung her head and scrubbed until her scarred hands wrinkled in the soap and water. While her hands remained busy, her mind churned over the conversation between Lord Dorrington and her uncle.

Her uncle had always been a driven and direct man. She heard her father and him argue many times over business and the legacy of the family name. Silly, innocent child she had been at the time, it never meant anything to her.

While her uncle always seemed cold and calculating, her cousin, Owen, proved quite charming and engaging, almost hedonistic in his pursuit of pleasure. They could not have been more opposite in her mind.

And what of Lord Dorrington? He seemed to be an enigma all his own. Lying to her uncle, keeping her presence a secret, yet somehow, she knew he would confront her. Would he punish her?

She set the pots aside and sighed, wiping her hands on her apron and brushing against the book. At least she could lose herself in another world...for a while. Reality seemed too harsh, and she knew Lord Dorrington would have her out on her backside for her indiscretion.

After closing the door behind Lord Longmont, Christopher turned and stared down the hallway. Irritation filled him. He was hardly surprised to find his study empty upon his return. Part of him wanted to ring for Jameson and have him summon Anne. He knew she heard part of his conversation with the viscount, but he could only presume she lingered there for the entirety of the exchange. How much did she hear? And even more important, how much did she understand?

He sighed and headed for the back of the house. The maid would have to be dealt with. However, she would have to wait. His conversation with Lord Longmont lingered in his mind.

Six months passed since his brother's death, and yet Magnus pushed to take his position as Viscount of Longmont, slipping so easily into his brother's title. The family barely took the time to grieve in a proper fashion.

Christopher pondered the questions Lord Longmont posed. They were not the gentle prodding curiosities of a family member. No, in all the years of his acquaintance with the Prescott family, he always sensed a drive and persistence behind anything Longmont showed an interest in. His history of dealing with the military and companies who provided raw materials for military production pegged him as a man of opportunity when it came to monetary gain.

And he wanted Christopher's metal.

Christopher shook his head. If only he still possessed it. He had not been lying when he said it was lost in the fire. Alistair and Christopher agreed to hide it away after the last failed experiment and attempted theft. Unfortunately, Alistair never told him where he put the metal for safekeeping. Christopher assumed it had been destroyed in the fire that killed his friend.

The servant's door led to the back garden, which then led to the small stable behind the house. He paused at the door, hearing the conversation of the servants echo up the staircase. The sound of laughter shook him from his musings.

At least he did something right when he hired Alistair's servants. Up until that point, he required one or two servants, but ensuring his friend's servants found suitable employment after the fire seemed to be the honorable path to take. Jameson and Margaret proved themselves invaluable. Elizabeth and Andrew were quite adept at their respective positions. It was too soon to adequately judge Anne's abilities as a housemaid.

His lips pulled into a frown. Something about her nagged at him. Her sad eyes and the mark of fire scarring her delicate face pulled at his heart.

He shoved the sympathy away. She had employment in his house and adequate pay. He could do no more for her. Although, he would have to address her eavesdropping. Such clandestine activities, however accidental, would not be tolerated.

He recalled the look of shock on her face when their gazes met. The horror of being caught froze on her parted lips and wide eyes. She looked like a terrified rabbit caught in a hunter's snare.

Longmont had been too self-absorbed, too caught up in his own conversation to notice the sudden burst of energy in the room. Bringing her into the moment would have been an error. One he knew would not set a good precedence.

Christopher nodded to himself as he pushed open the door and stepped out into the evening air. He would talk to her on the morrow after both of them took a moment to set their minds to a more stable state.

The garden seemed quite modest, he noted, as he crossed the cobblestone path cutting through the small, overgrown oasis. He made a mental note to have Jameson use the new steam clippers and tidy up the hedges and rose bushes. Perhaps he would have Andrew plant a few more items for Margaret to use in the kitchens. He was nothing if not practical. What good was a garden if you could not eat anything in it?

When he reached the stable, he opened the door and found Andrew sweeping hay from between the stalls. The building housed two stalls, a tack room, and a small sleeping chamber for the stable hand. While a larger, public stable resided just down the street, this private one suited his purposes just fine. It housed his two horses. He found no reason for a carriage, at least not yet.

"Good evening, my lord," Andrew greeted him and set the broom aside.

Christopher nodded to the lad.

"Would you like me to ready one of the horses?" The young man reached for the stall door. "I can have your gelding saddled in a flash."

"That will not be necessary, Andrew." Christopher held his hand out to halt the lad. "I wished to take a stroll and found myself here."

The truth was more complicated. He wanted to talk to one of the servants, any of them really, but he knew Andrew would be alone. Better yet, he was Anne's brother. And she happened to be the reason for his agitation at the moment, aside from Lord Longmont.

Andrew stepped aside as Christopher approached the stall door. His favorite horse, Mycroft, arched his neck searching Christopher's open palms for a treat.

"I am afraid I have no treat for you today, Mycroft, old boy." He smoothed his palm over the gelding's dark nose and up over the white blaze on his head. The dark red of his bay coloring gleamed in the dying sunlight from the open barn door.

"I have a nip or two, my lord," Andrew said handing over a few sugar cubes.

Mycroft snatched them from his open hand and munched away. Christopher gave the horse a solid pat on the neck before glancing at his body.

"You have been taking excellent care of my horses, young man." He turned to Andrew.

The young man's smile seemed hesitant but sincere. "I thank you, my lord."

"How long have you worked with them...horses, I mean?"

Andrew thought for a moment and shoved his hands in his pockets. "I started working with them when I was ten, my lord. My father worked as the stable master for Lord Longmont's family since he was a lad."

"He taught you everything you know then?" Christopher asked.

"Aye, my lord."

"And your mother, did she work for the Prescott's as well?"

The young man averted his gaze and moved to straighten the bales of hay stacked along the wall. "Aye, my lord, she served as the housekeeper for many years."

"You all served the Prescott family well. Your sister, Anne, is quite adept as a housemaid. I am honored to have you both serving in my house." The compliment served its purpose.

Andrew's head snapped up at the mention of his sister's name. "Has Anne gone and done something stupid?" His eyes narrowed.

Christopher arched a brow. What an interesting response. Was he concerned his sister would lose her employment? Had she done something in the past to warrant such a reaction from her brother?

"No, nothing of the sort." He watched Andrew shift his weight from foot to foot, his hands clenching by his sides. "She has done nothing wrong. It is mere curiosity on my part."

The lad's jaw tightened. "Curious, my lord?"

Ah, he thinks I have an interest in his sister. Best change direction. "The scars she bears. Those would have been quite horrific. Was she in the house the night of the fire?"

Andrew visibly relaxed, although his speech remained stiff. "Aye, she was...trapped in the house." The lad turned away for a moment before continuing, his voice thick with emotion. "I rushed into the blaze and pulled her out."

"I see." Christopher approached him. "And you were not

injured?"

"I have a few burns from the falling ash, but nothing compared to her...injuries." He paused before the last word, as though guilt wrapped itself around him.

"You saved her life," Christopher said clapping a hand on the lad's shoulder. "You should be proud of that."

Andrew nodded and stepped away. "If you would excuse me, my lord, I must return to my duties." The lad pulled on his cap and walked out of the stable.

Christopher stared after him. What a strange relationship he had with his sister. Almost as if he could not bear to speak of the incident or of her in general.

The sun set, casting long shadows against the buildings. Christopher walked toward the house lost in thought. He glanced up and caught sight of the flutter of a white curtain against the third story window. His bedroom window.

Once he reached his study, he collapsed in his oversized chair behind the desk. The room looked clean and tidy. At least Anne completed her task.

He glimpsed the corner of his folio sitting on the edge of the desk. Had it not been on the other side earlier? He shrugged as he pulled it close and opened it. The notes drew him in for a moment before he caught sight of one page covered in what he recognized as Alistair's handwriting. The date listed it as three days before the fire. These were the notes for the final experiment Alistair conducted on the metal. He removed the papers from the folio and set them aside. Turning to his bookcase, he searched the shelf for his personal journal.

As he slid the oversized journal from the shelf, Christopher noticed the empty space out of the corner of his eye.

His copy of *Wuthering Heights* was missing.

Chapter Four

The soft sound of Elizabeth snoring echoed in the dim room. A warm glow from the lantern lit the pages of the book, but Elizabeth's presence and the heavy weight of guilt sitting upon her shoulders weighed her down. She could not enjoy her novel...not a single word. The book fell in her lap and closed with a dull thud.

Elizabeth shifted in the bed beside her and mumbled unintelligible words before falling into a snorting slumber.

Adele never shared her bed before. The whole idea of it seemed foreign. But she would admit Elizabeth ensured her toes did not freeze during the night. Their small fireplace hardly kept the room well-heated, so having another person in bed with her fixed that problem.

Her current restlessness lay in her guilt more so than her current company. Deep in her heart, she pined for the comfort of her own room, her own bed, the cozy nest she used to make before curling under the blankets and opening the pages of a new novel. Nothing compared to those moments of true happiness.

Elizabeth's snore shook her from the happy memory and brought her right back into the moment of agonizing guilt.

Lord Dorrington had not sent for her after dinner as she assumed he would. Nor did he summon her at any other point in the evening. He dismissed them all when he retired for the night and disappeared into his chamber. Their master did not even spare her a glance as he passed her in the hallway.

The man must be devising some horrid punishment for her for having listened to his conversation with Lord Longmont. She knew she had been in the wrong. The first rule

Margaret instilled in her when they devised this plan to have her become a servant was quite clear. Servants are to be silent and invisible unless called upon.

Adele huffed. She never had been submissive child. In fact, her willful nature had been the primary reason her parents delayed her coming out. They wished for her to mature enough to ensure a proper match. No one wanted a willful wife, let alone a well-read and educated woman. A sinking sadness settled into her bones as the past months came back to her in a rush.

She glanced at the book in her hands and sighed. This would never do. She needed something with more fantastical settings, something that would whisk her away from the harsh reality of her daily life. As much as she loved a good mysterious romance, she longed for distant shores and undiscovered territory. Perhaps a pirate tale or one of Jules Verne's adventures would suffice.

Having made up her mind, Adele slipped from the bed and wrapped her heavy shawl around her shoulders. The whole house would be abed at this hour.

Adele tiptoed down the servant's stairs to the second floor. She came closer and noted the door stood ajar, a glow of light from the fire still evident, but dimmed. She lifted the lamp to better see her way and swung the door open.

The bookshelf stood against the far wall, dark and tall like a steadfast knight hidden in the shadows. Adele crept closer and found the empty spot where Wuthering Heights belonged. She replaced the novel and scanned the spines for an alternate selection. When she spotted the silver etching that read *20,000 Leagues Under the Sea*, a smile broke upon her lips. Adele removed it and cradled it against her chest with one hand while the other held the lamp aloft.

"I trust you will replace that book once you have finished it."

The book fell from her hand as the voice echoed behind her, dark and deep like the endless seas, roiling with dangerous depths. She turned to see Lord Dorrington sitting in the chair beside the fire with a half-full glass. The firelight glinted behind him, casting his features into shadow, but she knew it was him. She also recognized the smile that played on his lips. He caught her, twice.

Adele might as well return to her room that very moment and pack her belongings. She would not be welcome in the house after being willful and disobedient.

"I beg your pardon, my lord." She crouched down to retrieve the book and put it back on the shelf. As she spun around, Lord Dorrington stood before her.

She almost collided with him, he stood so close.

"My apologies, my lord." Adele dropped her gaze. "I should never have been presumptuous."

"For borrowing my books?" He blocked her escape. "Or for eavesdropping on my private conversation?"

Adele's heart stuttered and pounded twice as hard. She pinched her eyes closed, hoping the whole debacle would vanish like a nightmare upon waking. Her eyes opened. Lord Dorrington's brow rose, his expression unreadable. Yet she could tell by his posture he was not upset.

They stood toe to toe. Adele pulled her shawl tight around her body as if it could shield her from his heat. He studied her close. She found it more disconcerting than if he would have shouted at her and banished her from his home.

"I shall take my leave in the morning, my lord." Adele forced herself to meet his steady, unnerving gaze.

"No."

The solitary word slid from his tongue and dropped between them, rendering Anne speechless.

Christopher stared down at Anne. She seemed softer, more fragile in her nightgown and robe. Her dark hair trailed in a thick braid over her shoulder. A few escaped tendrils curled around her face and framed her expressive eyes. She dropped her gaze to the floor.

Her penitent reaction confirmed his decision. She knew the egregious error she committed. Honestly, Christopher found her penchant for reading to be a refreshing development. Most servants stole silver or sold secrets to petty thieves. However, this clever magpie relieved a book from his private collection. Not stolen, but borrowed, if her returning the first one was any indication.

Anne avoided his gaze. She shifted her weight from one foot to the other as though uncomfortable by his close proximity. He took a step back but still caged her in against the bookcase. The silence between them stretched thin. He waited to see if she would press for an explanation.

Finally, she looked at him. "Why will you not allow me to take my leave?" Her voice remained composed, but he noted the flare of irritation in her eyes.

"Because you intrigue me, Anne." He tapped his fingers on the glass in his hand.

"I...I intrigue you?" She looked worried, her gaze darting over his shoulder toward the door, toward an exit.

Christopher tisked. "Come now. I have no intention of seducing one of my servants." He turned to return to his seat by the fire. "Come join me a moment."

He glanced over his shoulder ensuring she followed him. Hesitation flickered in her expression and her movements, but she joined him beside the fire.

"Please, have a seat." He sat and gestured to the seat opposite him.

Anne lowered herself to the seat, her hands clasped demurely in her lap, her ankles crossed. She sat like a lady, not a maid.

Ideas began to form in the back of Christopher's mind. "You were Adele Prescott's maid, were you not?"

She blinked a few times, her lips pressing together before she spoke. "Yes, my lord. I served her for several years."

"Did no one notice how similar the two of you were?" he asked before adding. "In stature and coloring, I mean."

"Yes, my lord." She dropped her gaze to the fire, avoiding his scrutiny once more. "She often teased me about being the sister she never had."

Christopher's questions grew, but he did not wish to alarm or upset the young maid with his inquiry. "Anne, do you know of anyone who would have wished Lord Longmont ill or would have done something to hurt him or his family?"

Her eyes widened for a moment before meeting his. "Do you believe the fire was set intentionally, my lord?"

Her question caught him by surprise. He concealed it before responding. "I believe so," he said. "Although I cannot prove it."

She twisted her fingers in the edge of her shawl and chewed on her lower lip for a moment as if in thought. "Someone killed m — them on purpose."

He nodded and took a drink. The whisky warmed him as the ideas blossomed into a plan. A very dangerous deception that could put both of them in harm's way. Christopher studied the quiet young woman before him. With the right clothing and instruction, Anne could fill the role quite well. But he would never ask her to do something she was not comfortable undertaking.

"I have a plan, sweet Anne, but it requires your assistance." He set the glass aside and leaned closer.

"What plan?" she asked, hugging the shawl tighter around her body. "And why would you need my assistance?"

"I wish for you to impersonate someone."

Anne looked scandalized. "I...I am not sure this is wise, my lord."

"Please, just listen before you decide against it." Christopher wanted to reach for her hand to soothe the worry that seemed to be welling up inside her. Damn and blast, he never meant to upset her.

She stared at him, unblinking. "Very well, tell me what you propose."

"In a fortnight, Lord Longmont is hosting a magnificent ball. A ball to which I have received an invitation this very evening." He paused for a moment to gauge her reaction before continuing. She nodded, so he pressed on. "I wish for you to attend by my side as Miss Adele Prescott."

Anne gasped, her hand flying up to cover her mouth. "My lord," she stammered. "I cannot impersonate...her. Such a thing would be improper and scandalous."

"Every soul in London believes Adele Prescott perished in that fire, even the person who wished her family dead." Christopher watched as she soaked in every word. "If you were to become her, no one would discredit you. They would believe you were recovering all this time. Your appearance would scandalize the entire country."

"But what would this do beyond that?" Anne seemed to ponder the idea.

"This is where it may be dangerous," Christopher confessed. "Your reemergence into society as Miss Adele would draw out the villain who killed the Prescott family. You would help me capture the man who caused this." He reached out and touched her cheek. "The man who killed Adele." The gloves maintained some distance even though the action felt more intimate than he intended.

Anne's eyes drifted closed at his touch. He noticed the tears as they ran over her cheeks. She dashed them away with a swipe of her hand and turned to face the fireplace.

"What shall it be, Anne?" he asked with a soft, persuasive tone. "Will you help me?"

Silence met his question.

"I shall give you unfettered access to my library. All the books I own, you may read, and any you wish for, I shall buy for you." Christopher placed a tempting offer before her, knowing of the love she harbored for the written word. No servant would tempt fate by borrowing a tome from their master's library if they did not crave the comfort of the story lying within.

Anne turned to face him. "I will participate in your charade, but I will require a gown and the proper adornments if I am to play the part of a lady at a ball."

"Whatever you need, I shall provide it." He could not stop the smile. "I will ensure you have everything you require to become Miss Prescott."

Anne seemed taken aback at his words but composed herself. "As you wish, my lord." She stood. "I should retire."

"Yes, you should." Christopher also rose to his feet. "Tomorrow we shall discuss it further, after your chores, of course. I expect you to continue your duties as a maid, you understand."

She faltered for a moment before offering a small bow. "Yes, my lord. Good evening."

Christopher watched her leave and a mixture of dread, excitement, and uncertainty washed over him. He hoped this idea worked. It all hinged on them believing Adele Prescott still lived. If he could convince Lord Longmont that his niece survived the fire, then perhaps he could draw him out.

Magnus wanted the metal with a desperation so intense that he would kill for it. At least, that was how he always behaved when he visited Alistair and Christopher in the laboratory. Even after the tragedy, he sniffed around searching for any remains of it or the experiments they performed.

Christopher poured himself another drink and downed it in one swallow. "If I must coax you out, then I shall, you rat."

He would have answers, and closure, if it killed him.

Chapter Five

Adele stared at her plate. Even though her stomach yearned for substance, it roiled at the thought of food. She took a hesitant bite and chewed, barely aware of the conversation around her.

While her friends and fellow servants enjoyed their breakfast, Adele kept her head down avoiding their worried glances.

"Are you well, my dear?" Margaret asked. "You look as though you have not slept a wink, and you have hardly touched your food." The older woman clucked with concern and affection.

"She reads when she should be sleeping," Elizabeth added between bites.

Jameson watched in silent interest as the two women turned their gazes toward Adele. Andrew sat at the end of the bench, his attention fixed on his breakfast.

"What have you been reading?" Margaret set her fork down and wiped her mouth.

"A novel," Adele replied, purposefully being vague.

Margaret's eyes widened. "Tell me you did not steal a book from the master's study."

"I did not steal a book," Adele said in her own defense. "I borrowed one."

Margaret stood, bustling around the kitchen in a cleaning frenzy. "You are not a lady here, Anne. You are a servant in the house of Lord Dorrington. Even borrowing a book in such a secretive manner is grounds for dismissal."

Adele sighed. "It does not matter. He knows I borrowed a book. I returned it last evening, and he caught me replacing it."

Silence descended on the small group. When Adele looked up, all eyes focused on her. A sense of foreboding settled in the pit of her stomach. It was not the consequences of her borrowing a book that had her shaken, but the agreement to which she and Lord Dorrington came to the evening before. Dare she follow through with such an arrangement?

Margaret's voice cut through her thoughts. "And yet the master has said nothing of your borrowing one of his books to me."

"My apologies." Adele pushed her plate away and faced Margaret. "There may be a much larger issue at hand."

"Oh, sweet angels of mercy, did he force himself on you?" Margaret sat down beside Adele. "Tell me, child, did he harm you in any way?" Concern shone bright in her eyes.

"Of course not," Adele replied, anticipation bubbling in her chest. "He never laid a hand on me."

Jameson visibly relaxed, as did Margaret.

"What did he do?" Jameson asked, engaged by the conversation at this point.

"He offered me an opportunity. Lord Dorrington wishes for me to pretend to be Miss Adele Prescott," she said, cutting straight to the heart of the issue.

"He recognized you?" Margaret's eyes widened as her voice dropped.

"No, in fact, he believes I am Anne. He never paid me any mind when he visited my father. In fact, I doubt we ever shared more than passing salutations and common courtesies." Adele twisted the cloth of her apron. "But Anne and I did have a similar build and coloring. There were a few who found the similarities unbelievable."

"Aye, you and Anne were similar in many ways, even in your stubbornness and need for the written word." Margaret patted her hand in an effort to comfort her. "But why would he ask you to assume the identity you are trying to hide?"

"He believes the blaze was set on purpose." She took a

deep breath. "He believes, as I do, that my family was murdered."

Jameson and Margaret shared a long, solemn look. Elizabeth stared at her, open-mouthed, before snapping it closed and looking at her in shock. When Adele hazarded a glance at Andrew, his complexion seemed to have paled while his body tensed.

"So, he intends to use you as bait then? To draw out the murderer?" The disbelief on Margaret's face echoed in Jameson's expression. "You did not agree to such folly, I hope."

A wave of guilt washed over Adele. She dropped her gaze to the deep groove in the table. In the moment, amidst the cover of darkness, it seemed to be the only reasonable course of action.

Deep in her heart, Adele knew the fire had not been an accident. She knew someone set it with the intent to kill every soul in the house. Had she not fallen asleep in the library on the main floor, she would never have been rescued. The fire consumed the upper floors first. By the grace of God, she survived, albeit not unscathed.

"Sweet child," Margaret said with a heavy sigh. "Why would you agree to such a dangerous scheme?"

"Because Lord Dorrington knows what happened was not an accident, and I deserve to know the truth of that night." Adele's heart pounded and her breath quickened. Passion flared beneath her controlled exterior.

"Such a deception could get you killed. I am sure you are aware of this," Jameson added in his solemn tone.

"I am aware of the risks," she said with a look at each person in the room. They rescued her, protected her, nursed her, and lied for her. A stab of betrayal pierced her heart at the thought of going against their wishes. She held her breath, wondering if she had been too hasty in her agreement to undertake such a charade. How could she possibly take it back?

"She dug her grave, let her lie in it." Andrew spat the words in spite and pushed away from the table. He left the kitchen, heading for the stables without another word.

Adele stared after him until he vanished from sight. She turned to Margaret, Elizabeth, and Jameson. Her heart ached at the thought of disappointing the handful of people in the world who cared about her well-being. The more she thought on Lord Dorrington's plan, the more certain she became that it was the correct path for her to take.

"I still say it is too dangerous for you to undertake such a role." Jameson rubbed his hand along his jaw. "But if this is what you truly believe you need to do, then we will support your decision."

"Aye," Margaret added. "Your parents were strong, God fearing people. They deserve to have some peace, as do you, my dear. If this will help you through this difficult time, then do what you must."

"Am I to be the only maid again?" Elizabeth pouted. She smiled in an effort to break the tension hovering in the air. "We shall have to hire another then, I suppose."

Adele smiled at her friend. "I shall still help you around the house. Lord Dorrington never mentioned me giving up my duties completely. In fact, he never explained what my part will truly be in this production."

"Perhaps he will make that more clear this afternoon. Remember to be careful, Anne," Jameson said as he rose from his seat. "Now if you will excuse me, I must attend my obligations." He straightened his jacket and brushed his cuffs before exiting the room.

Margaret bustled around the kitchen preparing a morning breakfast to place in the dumbwaiter. As if on cue, Otis beeped from the opposite wall as his doors slid open.

"Infernal machine." Margaret glanced at her watch. "You are early." She jabbed her finger at him.

Elizabeth turned to Adele and clasped her hands in her own. "Did he even attempt to seduce you?"

Adele shook her head. "Not in the slightest. His intentions toward me seemed quite innocent."

Elizabeth nodded with relief before turning away. "I shall see to the main floor if you will make sure the fires are set in the upper rooms."

Adele had no time to process her friend's question before the moment passed. As she climbed the staircase to the second floor, Adele could not help but wonder. Lord Dorrington could not possibly view her in such a manner, could he?

The morning light stung his eyes when he opened the curtains in his bedchamber. Sleep eluded Christopher after his encounter with the maid in his study. She was a curious little thing. A strange, harebrained scheme stole his slumber. When the plan to have her impersonate Miss Prescott took root in his mind, he could not purge it. He turned the possibilities over and studied them, aiming for the best possible way to ensure their safety and yet set the perfect trap.

After she left him alone, he spent several hours going over the notes he and his partner compiled in regards to the metal and their experiments with it. Someone wanted it desperately enough to kill for it that much he knew. But who would have had ready access to the information they held?

One name came to mind — Lord Longmont. He often made it a point to visit his brother in his laboratory, even though it was often restricted to anyone besides himself and Alistair. The matter of the title, which Magnus often coveted in his actions and, in seldom occurrences, his words, rose to the forefront of his reasoning.

Christopher dressed. It took him months to learn how to use his new hand. A valet would have proven quite useful at such moments. However, since the accident in the laboratory, the thought of having someone touch him brought physical pain.

Neither he nor Alistair could quite understand the result of their failed experiment, but it left him with an ache burning deep, only to be compounded at the absence of any human touch.

No point dwelling on it. With a sigh, he finished preparing for the day.

He planned to spend the day in his study doing more research and formulating a strategy to convert the simple, yet sweet Anne into Miss Adele Prescott. She would need to play the part without hesitation. He was fortunate the women were acquainted at one point. It would make her transformation easier.

When he pulled open the door, he nearly collided with the young woman in question.

Anne pulled back and dropped into a hasty bow. "Please pardon me, my lord. I did not realize—" She snapped her mouth shut as if realizing her excuse was unnecessary.

"Anne," Christopher said in a soft tone. "I was about to send for you to join me. We have some details to discuss."

"As you wish, my lord." She dropped her gaze and followed him down the stairs.

He opened the door and gestured for her to enter his study first. The curtains had been drawn back, and a fire burned low in the hearth. A faint stream of sunlight shown through the window.

Anne stepped into the beam and the light radiated around her face, highlighting the delicate features.

Even though he could not remember Adele's features in vivid detail, Anne could very well be her twin, for their likeness seemed uncanny. The scars along her jaw did not detract from her beauty. They leant her an air of mystery and perhaps a hint of danger. He cursed his overactive imagination.

"Please, sit." Christopher gestured to the chair opposite his by the fire.

Anne sat, crossing her ankles and folding her hands in her lap, as a lady should.

"You blend seamlessly into the role of lady," Christopher commented in appreciation. "Teaching you the basic etiquette of society should prove to be quite simple."

The young woman seemed surprised by his observation. She averted her gaze.

"Have you changed your mind about becoming Miss Prescott?" he asked, sensing her hesitation.

"No, my lord." She met his gaze. Her bright eyes sparkled in the morning sunlight.

"Very well." He leaned back in his chair, and then saw the flash of hesitation and nervous avoidance again. "You have questions?"

She nodded. "I do."

"Proceed." He listened, both curious and intrigued by this woman before him.

"Do you truly believe my...Lord Longmont and his family were murdered?" she said, her attention focused on him.

"Is that what you believe, Anne?" he asked, careful of how to proceed.

"If the fire was set on purpose, then yes, I believe the intent was murder." She paused. "We all could have suffered the same fate as the family." Her voice dropped low in respect of the deceased.

"It is a possibility." He took a breath. "What do you know of Lord Longmont's, I mean, our work in the laboratory?"

Anne met his gaze, curious, and yet he caught the hesitation in her actions. "I am not aware of any of the details of the work Lord Longmont did in his laboratory. It was always off limits to the servants and the children."

Christopher nodded. "Then you have not heard any rumors surrounding his work?"

"None, my lord," Anne replied.

"Lord Longmont and I took on a project together." He took a deep breath and flexed his mechanical hand beneath the fabric of the glove as though it would stave off the memories. "His brother, Mr. Magnus Prescott, also took a keen interest in the substance we were studying.

"I spent months analyzing that material, and nearly killed myself in the process," he said. There was no reason to elaborate on the full consequences of his experiment's failure. "The delicate nature of the material and its temperamental qualities intrigued me, but both Alistair and I knew it could prove lethal if it fell into the wrong hands."

"The theft?" Anne murmured as though a thought just came to her out of the blue. "One evening after the family went out, the laboratory was sacked. All of Lord Longmont's belongings broken or destroyed." Her gaze fixed on his with the realization. "They were looking for the substance you were studying?"

Christopher nodded. "You wouldn't have happened to see anything that night, would you?"

Anne shook her head. "No, my lord. Elizabeth and I had already retired for the evening, but I remember the whirlwind of activity the next day. Lord Longmont was beside himself." She looked away. "I remember when you arrived and spoke to the late Lord Longmont."

She remembered him. He wished he could place her in his memories, but they were not as reliable as they once were. Especially since the experiment's failure.

"That day, Lord Longmont and I agreed that the experiments should stop, at least for a short time, until we discovered who raided his laboratory." Christopher flexed his hand again. "Unfortunately, a few days later, well, you know what happened." He paused, collecting himself. "You and the other servants were fortunate to have survived, Anne."

Her hand rose to her face. Delicate fingers skimmed over the pink scar tracing her jaw. He wanted to reach out and take her hand. Show her a bit of sympathy. He could see the sheen of tears in her eyes and the tremble of her lower lip. Clearly, there had to be something wrong with him. He cleared his throat.

After a few moments, Anne lifted her head and laid her hands in her lap once more. "Whatever became of the material? Was it taken?"

"That is one question to which I wish I knew the answer." Christopher stood and paced before the hearth. "I do not believe the thieves succeeded. I would have heard something within the scientific community. I have also had several inquiries as of late from the current Lord Longmont as to our experimental findings and the substance in question."

"Then it must have been destroyed in the fire," Anne said softly.

"It must have been," Christopher agreed. "Unless Alistair succeeded in hiding it. It seems to be a mystery to which we will never uncover the answer."

"Did he not give you some clue as to where he may have hidden it?" Anne asked.

"Unfortunately, no. We were to meet the morning following the fire and discuss the next steps in our partnership." Christopher sat down again, agitated by the unknown. He straightened his jacket. "Are you still willing to take part in my plan to draw out those who have acted against us?"

Anne pressed her lips together as if afraid of what might pass them without her permission. She turned toward the hearth, losing herself in the flames for a moment before facing him once more.

"I shall be taking part in a charade that will shock the whole of London society," Anne said. "What assurances do I have of my safety in such a deception?"

"On my honor, I shall remain by your side and keep you sheltered from any harm that might befall you." Christopher never made oaths, but in this moment, his desperation overcame any rational sense. He wanted answers, and having Anne play the part of Adele would bring him closure. "You have my word."

"I want more than just your word," she said matter-of-fact. "When this production has ended, I shall require a means of escape. Society has no tolerance for those who will play them for fools. You will grant me a small yearly allowance and provide a cottage for me in the country."

Christopher stared at her, startled and a bit surprised by the audacity of such a request. But it was not unreasonable. After all, he was placing her in harm's way. The least he could do was ensure a comfortable life for the woman who helped him solve the mystery that held him captive.

"You shall have it," he said with a small smile. "We have an accord then?"

Anne tilted her head in acknowledgement.

"We shall begin your training tomorrow then."

"What training?" she asked.

"You must emulate Miss Prescott in every possible way. Since you have spent your life as a servant in a lord's house, you know there are certain rules and etiquette one must follow as a member of polite society." He watched her reaction. "I must instruct you on how to be a proper lady."

Surprise filled him when she smiled. "As you wish, my lord."

"Very well." He cleared his throat. "In a fortnight, Lord Longmont will be hosting a ball. You will be attending as Miss Prescott. I am in hope this will draw our culprit forward to action."

"A lady believed to be deceased for months appears at her uncle's ball unannounced." She seemed to be lost in thought. "This will certainly cause quite a scandal."

"One can only hope for such a reaction," he replied. "By morning, all of London will be talking of Miss Prescott and her miraculous survival. If that fire was not an accident, then we shall know soon after Adele's emergence into society once more."

"This all sounds rather complicated." Anne shifted in her seat, uncrossing and re-crossing her ankles.

"It will work," Christopher promised.

"How can you be sure?" she asked.

"I just am." Honestly, Christopher was not sure. He hoped his inclinations were accurate. It had to be successful, but only with Anne's help could he be assured of it.

"Why do you care so much about this?" Anne glanced at him. "They were not part of your family. You owe them no loyalty. And besides, they are gone. What good will it do now?"

"They deserve justice," he said, his tone soft but stern.

"Why must you be the one to ensure it?" She tilted her head to the side.

"Because," he replied, "It was my obsession which caused their deaths." He stood and retreated to his desk. "That will be all for today, Anne. Please return to your duties. I shall call for you in the morning to begin your lessons."

"As you wish, my lord."

Christopher could not look at her. His conscience pricked at his chest, so he ignored it and picked up a letter from the tray.

When the door clicked shut, he collapsed into his chair and ran his hand through his hair. Uncertainty burrowed into his conscience. This was the right thing to do, was it not?

Chapter Six

Adele collapsed onto her bed. The day passed in a blur of activity. She kept busy for she knew if she stopped the unanswered questions would rise from the dark recesses of her mind and dissuade her from continuing forward in Lord Dorrington's plan.

Elizabeth entered the room and sat on the opposite side of the bed. "Are you feeling well?"

She nodded. "Why do you ask?"

"You hardly spoke during the evening meal, and I have never seen you work as hard as you did today." Elizabeth took off her cap. "Did something happen when the master spoke to you today?"

Adele sighed. "He is convinced there is someone to blame for my family's death." She paused. "And yet, he blames himself for it." She unwrapped her hair from the coil at her nape.

"Do you believe he had something to do with it?" Elizabeth asked.

"To tell the truth, I do not know what to believe." She set the pins aside and picked up the brush. "Why risk public scorn and have me pose as Miss Prescott? Why would he take us in as his personal servants when he had no responsibility for the servants of the late Lord Longmont?"

"Perhaps it is guilt he feels." Elizabeth took the brush from her hand and ran it through Adele's hair with gentle strokes. "He was a close friend of the family and partners of a sort with Lord Longmont. Mayhap he believes he could have done something to prevent such a tragedy." She paused for a moment before continuing. "I wish I could forget that horrid night."

"As do I." Adele relaxed as her friend continued to brush and then braid her hair.

An amiable silence fell between them before either spoke again.

"Do you believe Lord Dorrington had something to do with the fire?" Elizabeth asked, her voice low.

"I do not know." Adele pondered the possibility for a long while. It had been one of the primary reasons she took the position as a maid alongside Elizabeth. She had been sure before, but his offer stirred other possibilities in her mind.

"He would not go to such lengths as deception to draw out a killer if he was the perpetrator. Would he?" Elizabeth set the brush aside.

Adele stood and looked at her companion. "It does seem a bit excessive to undertake such a plot if that were the case." She tilted her head to the side. "However, I do believe he knows more than he admits. He has a bigger role in this."

Elizabeth helped her disrobe and don her nightgown. Even though they were equals now, Elizabeth always treated Adele as a lady in private.

Old habits are difficult to break.

The thought of resuming her old identity under the pretense of being the actual Miss Prescott struck her as almost ridiculous. These types of scenarios happened only in plays and novels, not in reality. What would Lord Dorrington say if he knew the truth of her identity?

A nervous laugh escaped her, catching Elizabeth unaware. The other girl startled, her eyes wide.

"My apologies," Adele said, covering her mouth with her hand.

"Something amuses you?" Elizabeth asked, turning to remove her own garments.

"Yes, actually, this whole situation seems almost like a Shakespearian comedy."

"What do you mean?" Elizabeth asked with true curiosity.

"Well, I find it quite amusing that Lord Dorrington would ask a maid to pretend to be a lady, and that in actuality the maid is truly the lady she is pretending to be." Adele gave another nervous laugh.

Elizabeth smiled, but she remained somber. "You are worried about agreeing to his scheme."

Adele sat on the bed as the worry and humor churned in the pit of her stomach, making her feel ill. "I would be a fool not to be concerned." She fidgeted with her braid. "The truth will undoubtedly come out when I appear at the ball with Lord Dorrington."

Her companion spun around to face her. "Lord Dorrington is escorting you to a ball?"

She nodded. "Yes, my uncle, the newly appointed Lord Longmont, is hosting a large gala in a fortnight. It is to be my grand appearance."

Elizabeth dropped onto the bed beside her. "That ball is to be the event of the season. The whole of London will see you there. This will not be a charade, it will be an unmasking."

"They will see what they want to see," Adele said with a heavy heart. "I will not reveal the truth should Lord Dorrington choose to reveal I am a maid in disguise."

"Why?" Elizabeth begged, "You could have your life and your place in society back."

"What good are those things when the ones you love have gone?" She hung her head. "No, I do not intend to stay in London after the ball." Adele twisted her hair around her finger. "Lord Dorrington has agreed to provide a comfortable cottage and yearly income. I have no intention of returning to society after this is over."

"He has agreed to such terms?" Elizabeth asked surprise etched on her face.

Adele nodded. "He has."

"When he discovers the truth, will he not force you to return?"

"He will never know." Adele took her friend's hand in her own. "You must tell the others not to betray my confidence."

"We will take your secret with us to the grave, should that be your wish," Elizabeth replied. "But we will support you in any way we can, even if you decide to become a lady once more."

"As soon as we uncover the man responsible for my family's death, Miss Prescott will no longer exist." She released her hand. "I will be free."

"If that is what you desire." Elizabeth smiled. "Goodnight, miss."

They climbed beneath the counterpane. Adele blew out the lamp and the room glowed with the light from the fire in the grate.

Adele clasped the pendant between her breasts, closed her eyes, and prayed. *Father, show me the way. Am I taking the wrong path? Help me, guide me.*

The pendant warmed in her hand, radiating a soothing heat. She held it tight as her mind faded into a dreamless slumber.

Christopher checked his watch for the third time before tucking it back into his waistcoat. He scheduled the appointment with the modiste for ten o'clock. They had a half an hour to make the appointment.

He sighed. Surely, he made the right decision in transforming Anne into Adele. Their resemblance aside, he could not delude himself into thinking he could change a maid into a lady. While her performance may be flawless, he worried she may draw undue attention to herself before the reveal. In fact, he decided against escorting her in public more than necessary.

He had Andrew hitch the team to the brougham he

rented to conceal them from curious onlookers. His frequent appearance in society would cause enough gossip. The last thing he needed was undue attention on his protégé imposter.

As he reached for his pocket watch again, he noticed Anne coming towards him. She wore a simple gown and a matching wrap. Her hat sat askew on her loose chignon. Anyone passing her on the street would never grace her with a second glance.

That summarization ended when her gaze met his.

Her eyes sparkled with intelligence and curiosity. With her head bowed, she maintained the humble stance of a servant, but when engaged, she would be a lady of magnitude, of that he could be positive.

Clearing his throat, he opened the door for her. "After you, my lady."

Anne gave a graceful tilt of her head before exiting the townhouse and descending the stairs to the waiting carriage.

Andrew held the door for her, aiding her ascension with his gloved hand. A look passed between them, one Christopher would have missed had he not been avidly assessing her movement and actions. They were siblings—perhaps a rivalry or concern for her safety. He would make it a point to speak to Andrew later that afternoon and assure him of Anne's safety.

He climbed into the carriage, situating himself beside her, but being aware to leave space between them. The last thing he needed was to touch her more than necessary. Every possible contact could increase his chances of a painful reoccurrence. He swallowed hard as the carriage lurched into motion.

Anne stared out the window as they made their way down the crowded street. Christopher watched her. She sat still, as if also afraid to touch him even by accident. Her lips pressed together when she turned and met his scrutiny.

"You wish to say something, Anne?"

She tilted her head, searching his face. "Where are you

taking me, my lord?"

"The modiste." He arched his brow at the look of uncertainty on her face. "The role of a lady requires the proper attire, does it not?"

Anne glanced down at her gown. "I suppose."

"And you require a gown for the ball, as well," he added. "Unless you would rather wear your uniform to the event of the season."

A small twist of her lips gave the hint of a smile. "I doubt that would serve your cause, my lord."

The carriage turned sharply. Anne leaned against him, their shoulders brushing at the motion. She straightened and mumbled an apology.

As much as he loathed admitting it, her fleeting touch of warmth brought a longing to the surface he had not felt in years. Having any form of companionship seemed foreign to him. He enjoyed his solitude, especially since returning from the war. The cacophony of noise and forced proximity to others made his head spin. Often the opium dulled the sense enough to keep his wits.

He licked his lips. Even though he visited the den only days before, he craved the sedation again. Although, oddly enough, Anne's company did not increase the desire for oblivion as others did. If anything, she curbed it. Odd, that.

They rode in silence until the carriage stopped in front of a fashionable shop on Bond Street. He avoided places such as this, lest anyone recognize him. However, he hoped the early hour would provide him a bit more anonymity.

Christopher stepped from the carriage and offered his hand to Anne. Her gloved hand slipped into his. She stepped down and released his hand as quickly as she had taken it.

Once he opened the door for her to enter the shop, the memory of the touch faded into the background.

Anne's attention skimmed the shop before being arrested by a woman approaching them wearing a delicate cream-colored gown.

"Good morning, how may I be of service, *madame*, *monsieur*?" Her subtle French accent and pleasant voice offered a welcome distraction.

"Good day." Christopher nodded in greeting, removing his hat. "My sister has an appointment with Madame Potter at ten o'clock."

Anne's gaze snapped to meet his, her eyes narrowed for a moment before a look of understanding crossed her features.

"Of course, *monsieur*." The woman turned her attention to Anne.

Christopher refused to correct the woman's assumption of his status. He wished for anonymity, of which this establishment assured. The less they knew, the better the situation would remain under his control. Besides, when one provided a bit of monetary incentive, all sorts of doors opened and questions remained unasked.

"We require four day gowns, two evening gowns, and a fine ball gown, as well as the necessary undergarments and outer garments." Christopher added as the woman took inventory of Anne in her small notebook. "Ready-made gowns should suit for the former, but the latter requires something custom and unique. Something to flatter my sister's fine complexion."

Anne stared at him, her eyes conveying what her voice could not. Fear and disbelief.

"Also, if my sister wishes for any other items, please have them added." Christopher smiled.

"Very well, *monsieur*." The modiste smiled and motioned to a side room. "If you will wait here, I shall take your lovely sister to be fitted immediately." She motioned for Anne to follow her.

Without a backward glance, Anne disappeared into the dressing room. He knew their return to his townhome would be rife with her dissatisfaction. Every nervous twitch of her body belied the truth. She wanted nothing from him outside of their agreement. But how was she to become Miss Adele Prescott without the proper wardrobe. Even she could understand the necessity of such expenditures.

He shrugged and pushed the thoughts aside as he took a seat in the gentleman's sitting room. Withdrawing his own personal notebook, he began outlining plans for Anne's next few lessons.

After an hour, the modiste returned wearing a glowing smile. "Your sister is ready, *monsieur*."

Christopher tucked his notebook away and joined the modiste and Anne in the main room.

Anne wore a becoming day gown. The cream and light blue highlighted her fair complexion without drawing too much attention. The cut flattered her figure, accenting her curves and bringing an undeniable touch of delicate femininity. His mouth went dry. This could not be the same girl who served in his home. She no longer looked like a maid, but a bonafide lady of status.

A hint of blush stained Anne's cheeks at his obvious perusal of her new garments. She turned her attention away, avoiding his gaze. A blossom of pride swelled in his chest. Anne proved a fine choice for his Adele.

Your Adele? He mentally shook himself. Such thoughts would come to nothing. He cleared his throat and turned away from Anne.

"You have outdone yourself, *madame*." Christopher complimented the proprietor.

"I shall have the rest of the garments delivered per your request, *monsieur*." The modiste bowed with a graceful smile.

"Come along, darling sister," he said as he offered his arm.

Anne thanked the modiste and took his arm. Together they exited the small shop and stepped out into the late morning air.

The carriage stood waiting for them. Andrew's eyes grew wide at the sight of Anne in her new gown. He quickly sobered and aided her into the carriage without a word.

"Take us home via the park, would you, Andrew," Christopher said to the young man as he stepped into the carriage.

"Aye, my lord." He closed the door and climbed into the driver's seat.

Christopher settled next to Anne and hazarded a glance in her direction.

The only things that changed were her garments, and yet Christopher sensed a renewed aura around Anne, as though the way she dressed transformed her state of mind. She sat straighter, her chin tilted higher, and even her mannerisms echoed a lady and not the maid he knew her to be.

She turned, meeting his bold attention. "I hope my appearance does not displease you, my lord."

He cleared his throat. "On the contrary, the transformation is astonishing."

This time she blushed. "I am pleased it meets with your approval." She pulled at the gloves. "Although I do not see the need for so many gowns, when the only event I shall be attending is the ball."

"A lady must be prepared." He watched as she toyed with the fringe on her gown.

"Thank you."

Her words gave him pause. He had not anticipated her gratitude to please him as it did. All he could do was nod in reply.

"May I ask you a personal question, my lord?"

He nodded and attempted to calm the anxiety from rising. *What madness is this?*

"I have noticed you wear gloves all the time," she observed. "Even when you are home working in your study. Why?"

Christopher hesitated for a moment before answering. Only one person knew the truth behind the gloves. So, he chose to share half the truth and removed the glove covering his prosthetic hand. The metal and intricate gears lining the back of his hand and down the length of his fingers glinted in the light.

Anne's soft gasp drew his gaze up to gauge her reaction.

Before he could react, she removed her glove and traced the copper wires along the back of his hand where they disappeared into the intricate gears.

Christopher watched in fascination as her fingertips grazed his metallic hand. A pang of longing shot through him. His eyes drifted closed for a moment as he imagined the feel of her skin against his, even in such an innocent touch as this. His hand flexed beneath hers.

Nothing.

An objection died in his throat as she lifted his hand and turned it over between hers, inspecting the craftsmanship. It had been a prosthetic of his own design. With the help of Alistair, they perfected the mechanism allowing it to function just like a real appendage.

"Why would you keep such a work of art hidden away from the world?" she said, her voice a mixture of awe and admiration.

Christopher snatched his hand away and replaced the glove, hiding it once more. "I created it to function, not to be put on display." He winced at the harsh tone of his response.

Her excitement dashed by his remark, she pulled on her gloves.

They traveled in silence for a few minutes before she spoke again. "How did it happen?"

He sighed. "I injured it in Khartoum while stationed with the army. The doctors could do nothing to save it."

She nodded in understanding and rested her gloved hand on his sleeve.

Christopher struggled to maintain his composure. Never in his life had he wanted something as much as he wanted to accept her sympathy, her touch. Instead, he pulled away knowing the consequences of such a longing.

"When we return, you may return to your duties. We will resume our lessons tomorrow." Christopher's brusque and concise instructions signaled the end of the discussion.

"Yes, my lord." Anne's clipped response stung.

How easily they fell back into their respective roles. Christopher noted the cold indifference in her expression as she stared out the window.

The carriage pulled to a halt before his townhouse. He stepped from the conveyance and offered his hand. Anne climbed from the carriage, pointedly ignoring his offer of aid and brushing past him toward the entrance of his home.

Christopher should have experienced relief at the distance between them but regret and longing consumed him long after he returned to his study.

Chapter Seven

Adele cut the vegetables according to Margaret's instructions. Several days passed in a blur of work mixed with various, sporadic lessons with Lord Dorrington during the day. She could not help but smile to herself. Every instruction, every example set forth by Lord Dorrington served as a vague reminder. Of course, she excelled with exemplary ease.

Once a lady, always a lady, even if it was only at heart. Adele learned to be a housemaid, and in the same way she learned to be a proper lady. Retaining such instruction did not prove to be problematic in the slightest. A small burst of pride swelled in her chest. Becoming Miss Prescott would not be a difficult feat.

However, maintaining her composure around Lord Dorrington grew more challenging with every passing lesson.

She attended to her task, ignoring the chatter between Elizabeth and Margaret. Her mind drifted to the moments they shared during the return carriage ride from the modiste.

Her curiosity and unabashed boldness broke a small crack in Lord Dorrington's façade. But her small victory had been short lived. Their stolen moment had all but been forgotten when he summoned her the next morning for their first lesson. The calculating lord once again shuttered himself from her as he had the rest of the world, much to her disappointment.

She recalled the feel of his mechanical hand beneath her fingers and the intricate detail of the mechanisms that allowed him full movement of his hand. Adele saw a glimpse of the man beneath the indifferent exterior when she touched him. The moment lasted mere seconds, and yet a small bloom of hope sprang from it.

Until she walked into his study the following day and all traces of that man she glimpsed had vanished.

Adele arranged the vegetables on a tray to be roasted in the oven. Her mind churned. Had she overstepped in asking him such a personal question? She crossed a line when she touched him, inspecting his hand as though it were a trinket in a shop.

What a simple fool, treating him in such a way, she chastised herself as she worked. Their partnership in this venture was nothing more than a means to an end. For her, justice for her family and her freedom sat gleaming like a golden treasure at the end of a dangerous quest. Lord Dorrington meant nothing to her.

It mattered not to her who held her father's title or what material possessions she lost in that fire. She cared not who attempted to steal her father and Lord Dorrington's precious scientific experiment. Revealing herself to society would not bring back her family or restore her place in London's ranks, but it would draw out someone who knew what happened that night.

She craved answers. An explanation and swift justice. If Lord Dorrington could grant her that with his deception, then it would all be worth it.

A soft ache settled in her chest. Adele pushed it away. Sentimental attachments could prove disastrous. Even if Lord Dorrington showed an inclination toward her in such a regard, she would rebuff him. His enigmatic personality might seem charming to some, but to her, it confirmed her suspicions. She could not trust a man who kept secrets, and Adele knew everyone had them.

The soft beep and flicker of light from the communication device in her corner of the kitchen caught her attention. Wiping her hands on her apron, she approached it with apprehension.

Jameson taught her how to use the complicated contraption, but Adele avoided it if she could. Elizabeth and

Margaret were occupied at the moment, leaving Adele with no choice but to answer the call.

She lifted the cap on the receiver and pressed the green button.

"This is the kitchen," she said into the tube.

"I shall take supper in the dining room this evening." His voice echoed through the tube with disturbing clarity. "And set an extra place at the table as well."

"Yes, my lord," Adele replied, and the connection was severed.

"I wonder who he has invited over for dinner," Elizabeth said with an excited chirp as she carried a large serving platter to the table in the center of the room. "Lord Dorrington never invites anyone to dine with him."

"Never?" Adele found herself curious at the odd request.

"No, and this is the first evening he has instructed his supper to be served in the dining room. Most nights he takes a tray in his study." Margaret joined them as they readied the food in the serving dishes.

"Perhaps Mr. Prescott will be dining with him this evening," Elizabeth said with a sigh. "He cuts quite a dashing figure, does he not?"

"If I were a lady and twenty years younger, I would set my cap on him," Margaret said with a laugh.

Adele said nothing and smiled in agreement. The mention of her cousin in such a way made her pause. She always considered him charming and handsome, but he never struck her as the type of man to which she would find herself attracted. Even though they were cousins, he seemed to avoid her company whenever he visited. Congenial and superficial greetings for the most part.

When they were younger, they played together when he spent his summers with her family. But that had been years ago. Owen was at least eight years her senior. She was but a child when he last spent any real time with her.

The memories of her joyful childhood spent in the

country with her parents and brother threatened to drown her. She pushed away the ever-present grief and focused instead on her task.

Changing her apron and fixing her cap took a few moments, but the task sobered Adele. She resumed her role as dutiful servant to Lord Dorrington.

"I shall prepare the dining room," Adele said before gathering the necessary supplies to take upstairs.

She lost herself in the menial task. She set the china, arranged the silver, and placed the crystal glasses next to each setting.

A few minutes later, a melody of beeps sounded from the wall behind her. Otis' doors slid open revealing several of the larger serving platters. She removed them from his compartment and placed them on the buffet table.

"Thank you, Otis," Adele whispered to the machine.

As if in reply, he beeped twice before the doors slid closed.

"Were you talking to that machine?" Elizabeth asked from the far side of the room where she entered carrying a large tray laden with smaller serving dishes. "You cannot deny it. I saw you talking to Otis."

Adele hurried over to help her set the remaining food alongside the main dishes. "And what if I am? Will you say I am mad and have me committed?"

Elizabeth chuckled. "Never. We all talk to him from time to time. Well, everyone except Jameson. He is still upset Otis nearly took his fingers."

Adele smiled. She saw the animosity Jameson harbored toward the dumbwaiter. A quite ridiculous notion, to be sure, but Adele could not be sure Otis was wholly inanimate. Odd creation, he proved to be.

As they added the finishing touches, the door behind them swung open.

Adele and Elizabeth spun around to find Lord Dorrington standing in the doorway. They stood at attention, their heads bowed as they waited for their instructions.

"Elizabeth, would you please inform Jameson we are ready to eat. You may help him serve us this evening." Lord Dorrington assumed the seat at the head of the table.

"Very well, my lord," Elizabeth replied before exiting the room.

"Anne, please sit." He gestured to the empty seat she arranged across from him.

Adele paused, her mind spinning. Surely, he did not expect her to join him for dinner.

Her hesitation sparked a hint of irritation in his tone. "Miss Prescott, would you please join me for supper?"

Their gazes met, sparking for an instant before Adele sat down. He enjoyed toying with her. After all, he gave no indication she would be dining with him. Then she realized it was another lesson.

"You could have informed me of your intentions so I could have been more aptly prepared for tonight's lesson." Adele drew the napkin across her lap as she settled into the role of lady at a dinner party.

His brow rose at her comment, his gaze following her actions. "It seems as though you recovered well enough from the abrupt invitation."

Elizabeth and Jameson entered the room before she could reply. Elizabeth's eyes widened at the sight of Adele sitting at the table with Lord Dorrington, but she sobered as they took their positions beside the table.

"Let us begin, shall we?" Lord Dorrington placed his napkin across his lap.

Adele refused to be intimidated by his obvious challenge. If he wished for her to become a lady, then she would rise to the occasion.

A small smile stole across her lips. Lord Dorrington would find her to be an adept student, of that she had no doubt.

The woman opposite stunned him into silence. He had not anticipated her smile, or the easy acquiescence of such a brusque invitation. Part of him hoped to catch her off guard with this impromptu dinner lesson. However, she recovered in a moment, slipping from maid to lady seemingly without effort.

Her smile stole his ability to speak. He nodded to Jameson to begin serving the meal. The two servants moved with quiet efficiency. His attention, however, remained on Anne.

She waited, her gaze focused on the floral arrangement in the center of the table. Once she received the soup, she looked to him before retrieving her spoon.

Christopher ate his soup, encouraging her in his actions to follow suit. Together, they ate in silence, every course as quiet as the last.

He had never been much for idle conversation, especially at the dinner table. So, he searched for some small pieces of advice to bestow upon the lady before him, and yet he could find no fault in her behavior. The amount of time he spent in her company over the last few days enlightened him to her manners and etiquette. They were above reproach. However, it also reaped unintended consequences.

His gaze lingered on her. He could not help but notice the soft swell of her lips as she raised the crystal to her mouth tasting the sweet red wine. Her eyes fluttered closed. He tore his gaze away, craving much more than a simple meal of braised mutton and roasted vegetables.

"Does the wine agree with you?" he asked, desperate for conversation to distract him from his wayward thoughts.

"Yes, my lord," she replied.

Christopher leaned back, allowing Jameson to take his plate. He found he had no stomach for dessert. He waved the plate away when Jameson presented it.

Anne, however, accepted the dish with a look of pure bliss. Her cheeks pinkened, her mouth parted in delight, and her eyes feasted on the delightful chocolate confection placed before her. She glanced up before indulging.

"Are you not enjoying dessert, my lord?" she asked with a hint of surprise.

"I find I am quite satisfied with my meal." He motioned for her to continue. "Please, do not stop on my account."

She tucked in and lifted a small forkful of chocolate to her mouth. When it touched her tongue, Christopher all but groaned at the blissful expression transforming her face to one of orgasmic delight.

He summoned every ounce of restraint he possessed to remain impassive. His fist tightened around the napkin in his lap.

Every bite she took became overtly sexual. At least in his mind it did. Christopher was unsure how he controlled himself as he watched her devour her dessert. She savored every last bite. His body tensed and parts of him he long abandoned woke with renewed hunger.

He wanted dessert, of that he was certain. But no cake, no trifle, no decadent confection could tempt him the way the sweet, innocent Anne did.

Christopher blamed their interaction in the carriage for setting such an attraction ablaze deep in his chest. The way she touched him without repulsion. The way she gazed at his hand with admiration. How he longed for her caress. Not against his mechanical hand, but his flesh. Such desire would only prove disastrous, and yet it smoldered over the past few days. Every interaction with Anne fanned the flames hotter and brighter.

The game he played with her could be much more dangerous than he originally assumed.

When she finished the last bite, Christopher could have sighed in relief. She set her fork down and allowed Elizabeth to remove the dish. Satisfaction emblazoned itself on every one of her features. A sudden stab of jealous longing made him wish he had given her such an expression and not some damned dessert.

He pushed back from the table and stood. "Shall we adjourn to the study?"

Anne seemed a bit confused by the request and hesitated for a moment before joining him. "As you wish, my lord." She rested her hand on his proffered arm.

Beneath the cacophony of battling aromas, her sweet, warm scent teased him. Whatever attraction sparked during dinner blossomed into a fully-fledged wildfire. The heat of her touch sank deep through the layers of fabric settling into his bones. It seemed natural to have her on his arm. He noted the elegant way she carried herself as he led her through the house.

He escorted her to his study and abandoned her to close the door behind them. Christopher maintained a reasonable distance. Being near her much longer would well and truly make him forget himself and their mission.

Christopher turned his back and poured a glass of port for both of them. "I trust you enjoyed the meal?" He offered her one of the glasses.

She took it with a smile. "I did. My thanks for the invitation."

He leaned against the table and sipped the ruby liquid. "You, sweet Anne, are quite the enigma."

"Is that so, my lord?" she asked, avoiding his gaze.

"You take to this challenge like a fish takes to water." He regarded her closely. "I could never have expected you to learn so quickly with such little instruction."

"I have been around lords and ladies all my life." She paused before continuing. "Perhaps imitation comes naturally to me."

"A woman with such talents could easily fall into other employment opportunities. The theatre perhaps." He prompted her. It was true, with her ability to revert between such stations. She could be a great presence on the stage.

"I have never been to the theatre, my lord." She sipped her port.

"Pretending to be something you are not," he pondered. "Perhaps you missed your calling, my dear Anne."

Her eyes sparked with intelligence when their gazes met. "We have our agreement, my lord. All I wish for is a quiet, simple life. Nothing more."

"And yet the role you have agreed to play will make you the sensation of the season." He finished the liquid and set the glass aside. "The Resurrection of Miss Prescott. Has quite a lovely ring to it."

Anne set the glass on the mantle. "If you have quite finished, my lord, I have duties to attend."

He nodded, disappointment settling into his chest. *Damn it to hell.* Such an attachment could prove dangerous if it grew.

Before Anne could reach for the door, a knock shattered the silence between them.

"Come in," Christopher called wondering who would be intruding on his solitude this evening.

The door opened revealing Jameson and Owen.

"Mr. Prescott to see you, my lord."

Anne stepped to the side, her head bowed as Owen entered the room.

"Evening, old chap. Fancy a night out?" Owen asked with his usual boisterous charm.

Christopher could never manage to meet his enthusiasm or grace. They seemed to be opposites when it came to personality. He preferred a relaxing evening at home to Owen's propensity for nocturnal entertainment. And yet, they both enjoyed weekly visits to the Floating Den.

Owen glanced behind him, noticing Anne who now stood beside Jameson. "Am I interrupting something?" he asked with a wicked grin.

"Not at all." Christopher turned his attention to Anne

and Jameson. "That will be all."

After the two servants took their leave, Christopher sighed in exhaustion, pouring himself another drink.

"Would you like one?" he asked his guest.

"Yes, please." Owen came beside him and accepted the glass. "Cheers." He raised it in a toast and then took a drink once Christopher reciprocated the movement.

"Damn, but that maid seemed familiar," Owen observed. "Where did you pick her up?"

Christopher forced himself to remain impassive. Adele was Owen's cousin, after all, he would recognize her if given the right opportunity. Or he would reveal her for an imposter. "I took in all the servants who worked for your uncle. Do you not remember?"

"Ah, yes. I called you a damn fool for hiring the lot of them." He took another drink. "What was her name again?"

"Anne." Christopher ignored the jealousy rising like bile in the back of his throat.

Owen nodded. "Yes, now I remember her. Lovely little bit of lace, that one."

The unspoken implication lay perfectly clear. Owen could charm the undergarments off a nun. It should not come to any surprise he would seduce a maid. Jealousy roiled inside him.

"I would appreciate you abstaining from seducing any of my servants, Prescott." Christopher's grip tightened on the glass.

Owen turned toward him and laughed. "Of course. I have my sights set on another lovely, more eligible lady, remember?"

Christopher nodded steering the conversation away from Anne and her passing affair with Owen. "I do. You mentioned her fondly. How fares the hunt?"

"I shall have her, though hell should bar the way." Owen grinned.

"She has made you a poet, no less." Christopher smiled.

"Such a state of affairs must be quite serious for you to set your cap so firmly."

Owen sighed. "I shall make my intentions known soon enough." He set his empty glass aside. "Shall we make our escape then?"

"If you insist," he replied, setting his own glass on the table. "The club or the den?"

"Both." Owen smiled again, charm and wicked intent oozing from his very demeanor.

"Lead on." Christopher gestured toward the door.

As the men made their way down the stairs and gathered their outer garments at the door, Christopher found his mind returning to the sweet, yet tarnished Anne. He shook his head. If he remained in this house a moment longer, he might do something he would come to regret. As much as this new information should not influence his impression of her, it did. He wondered what other secrets she may be hiding beneath those seemingly innocent eyes.

They stepped out into the cool spring air and Owen hailed a cab.

Christopher glanced up at the house behind him. A figure disappeared behind the curtain on the third floor. *Anne.*

The allure of the Floating Den called to him. His emotions tangled in knots. He needed to refocus on the true nature of their association, to draw out the villain who ruined his life and killed his partner. She took the stage as a pawn. Yet, the image of her at dinner that evening haunted him during the ride to the club.

Even Owen's quick wits and candid stories could not distract him from the ache in his chest and the desire pounding in his veins. The club lost its appeal and the two men found their way to the Floating Den.

When he found solace in the opulent velvet rooms of the Floating Den, wrapped in the warm embrace of the smoke and mindless oblivion, Christopher could bury the

undeniable truth.
    He desired Anne.

Chapter Eight

Andrew glared at her from across the table during their morning meal. He sat in sullen silence while they ate. Margaret and Jameson discussed the minute details of the household schedule while Elizabeth and Adele engaged in a quiet exchange.

Elizabeth seemed oblivious to Andrew's pointed looks. Adele, however, felt the weight of his stare and the fury behind them.

She glanced at him and met his intense blue eyes.

He scowled deeper, if that were possible. The lines etched across his forehead contrasting with the deepening downward tilt of his lips. His ire toward her increased since she began her lessons with Lord Dorrington. He made a point of expressing his distaste for her without a word every time their paths crossed.

Adele could take it no longer. "Have you something to say to me, Andrew?" She set her fork down and stared at him. "Have I offended you in some manner?"

"Aye," he replied with a sneer. He shoved away his plate and stood. Without another word, Andrew headed toward the door leading to the garden and the stable beyond.

Jameson, Margaret, and Elizabeth all stared at Andrew until he disappeared. Their gazes then shifted to Adele who sat in stunned silence.

Finally, the irritation became too overwhelming. She would talk to him, at least to maintain they were in accord over the current situation. The last thing she needed was Andrew revealing her secrets to Lord Dorrington.

When Adele rose from her seat, Margaret spoke. "Go easy on him, my dear. He still has not been able to grieve properly."

Adele nodded in understanding and followed Andrew outside. When she reached the stable, she called out to him. "Andrew!" Her voice echoed off the rafters.

One of the horses nickered in response.

She sighed in frustration. Where could he have gone?

He appeared at the far end of the building when he stepped from the last stall. A thick lock of dark hair fell across his face as he brushed the hay from his trousers.

Their gaze locked. He folded his arms across his chest and cocked his head.

"Can we speak for a moment?" she asked in an attempt to be civil.

"Some of us have actual work to do," he snapped.

She approached him, not wanting to shout across the length of the stable. He stiffened as she drew closer and narrowed his eyes in distaste.

"What have I done to earn such scorn from you?" she asked. "From the moment I began my employment here, you have done nothing but look down on me with contempt and spite."

"What have you done?" he repeated with a mocking laugh. "As if you did not already know the answer to that ridiculous question." He leaned closer. "You survived while my sister died. Your presence is a constant reminder of that."

Adele's heart ached for him. She never intended for her assumption of his sister's identity to hurt him so deeply. Her words needed to be chosen with care lest she antagonize the grief more than necessary.

"I am truly sorry for your loss." She began. "It was never my intention to cause you such pain. But you were not the only one to lose your family in that fire." Her own heart sank like a stone at the memory of that night and its toll on both their lives.

He pressed his lips together in a thin line before dropping his arms to his sides. "You are playing a dangerous game."

She shook her head in confusion. Was he referring to her deal with Lord Dorrington? Or pretending to be a maid? "What—"

Andrew's response cut her off. "Do you take him for a fool?" He crowded her.

She backed away, her hands trembling with fear and anger.

"Lord Dorrington is not a simple man. He will uncover the truth." Andrew reached out and touched a lock of hair that fell from her topknot. "The dye is fading."

She stood transfixed and speechless. "Will you reveal it then?" Adele asked. "Will you tell him who I really am?"

He dropped his hand. "He will discover it without my interference."

"How can you be so assured?" Adele studied his face. Andrew always had been a handsome youth, but these last few months put a marked edge on his features, making him look rougher, darker, and even more attractive, if possible.

"Lord Dorrington keeps everyone at a distance. He avoids society and rarely ventures out except to visit his club or the den." Andrew's observations resonated with Adele. "And the only regular visitor he has is Mr. Prescott." The name slipped from his tongue on a hiss.

"You dislike my cousin?" she asked, remembering the evening before when he almost discovered her.

"Your cousin," Andrew spat, "Blinded my sister with his charms and then discarded her when he no longer desired her."

Adele gasped. "He seduced her?"

Andrew did not reply. Instead, he glanced at the stall beside him where a ginger gelding stood waiting for his feed.

"How can you be sure—" she began, but he spoke before she could finish her question.

"They are all the same. Bloody toffs think they are entitled to whatever catches their fancy." He met her gaze again.

Adele pondered his words. Being a servant illuminated her world in a new light, but she had not considered the possibility of being seduced by her employer.

"Now, go, leave me to my work." Andrew turned his back to her.

Without thought, she reached out and grabbed his wrist. "I—"

"Andrew, if I might have a word."

Lord Dorrington's voice startled her, and she dropped her hand, releasing Andrew from her grip.

She spun to see Lord Dorrington standing in the doorway. Her heart pounded. Had he heard their conversation? A sudden dread filled her.

Adele glanced at Andrew before turning to leave. His mask of dutiful servant slid into place.

"If you will pardon me, my lord." She bobbed a small curtsey before taking her leave.

Lord Dorrington's gaze followed her. She passed him, careful to avoid eye contact and refraining from bolting back to the house and locking herself away in her room.

Once she reached the kitchen, she pressed a hand to her chest and stopped to catch her breath. Adele willed her heart to cease pounding. There was no possible way Lord Dorrington could have heard her conversation with Andrew.

Each breath she took slowed the racing thoughts and the thundering of her heart.

Seeing Lord Dorrington gave her a fright, but it also unlocked strange feelings deep inside of her. She remembered the way he looked at her during their dinner lesson. The slight glimpses she stole in his direction made her curious as to his thoughts. With every bite of her dessert, his expression darkened. When he challenged her in his study after the meal, she nearly lost her composure.

Owen's arrival saved her, and yet it unleashed a whole flurry of concerns. If he saw her again, he would recognize her. They were blood after all. And knowing that Anne had more intimate relations with Owen made her feel ill. The thought of being seduced by him repulsed her.

However, the thought of Lord Dorrington seducing her set her heart racing. She leaned her head against the wall and closed her eyes. Such a multitude of conflicting emotions raged through her. Adele shoved them away and opened her eyes.

After collecting the rag and polish from the closet, Adele proceeded to the dining room to help Elizabeth with the silver. Before she reached the top of the stairs, a familiar voice stopped her.

"Anne, please join me in my study."

Adele turned to see Lord Dorrington standing near the door leading to the garden.

With a nod, Adele followed him down the hallway and up the main staircase.

What could he want to say that he needed to speak to her in private? She worried, drawing her lower lip between her teeth.

When he closed the door behind her, she inhaled, drawing in his scent as he brushed past her. The aroma of sandalwood and a hint of something sweet clung to him.

"Anne," he said, clasping his hands behind his back. "Is there something you wish to tell me?"

She stood tall and straight, motionless like a statue, with her head bowed.

Christopher rounded her, taking care not to draw too close. He went to the stables to give Andrew instructions for that evening. Instead, he stumbled upon the young man arguing with his sister. While their words were muted, the obvious tension between them spoke clear enough.

"No, my lord," Anne replied to his question.

What question? Lost in his own thoughts, he momentarily forgot but covered the lapse. "It has come to my attention that you were well acquainted with Mr. Prescott."

Her gaze snapped up, eyes bright and sharp. "Yes, my lord. It was but a passing fancy, I assure you."

"Lord Owen has led me to believe it once was more than a mere fancy." He raised his brow. How delicate could he put it?

"Whatever history Mr. Prescott and I had, it is quite firmly in the past." She glanced away for a moment before tilting her chin higher and facing him again.

"Very well," Christopher replied. While he disliked the idea of Anne with anyone, including his closest friend, he could not control her past, much like he could not control his own. All one could do was allow it to shape wiser decisions in the future. "Allowing yourself to learn from your past mistakes is an admirable quality, one I prize in my servants." He tilted his head. "Do I make myself clear?"

"Yes, my lord," she responded.

He said the words without actually saying them. The prospect of this conversation kept him up half the night, even with the pulse of opium in his veins. Christopher had never been one for confrontation unless it proved an absolute necessity. The thought of her with Owen strangled his relationship with his friend.

Owen had always been charming and flirtatious. It should not have surprised him to discover his friend seduced a maid. In fact, he would wager Owen seduced many servants in his years. Christopher envied Owen's easy ability to converse with women. A tendril of jealousy wove its way through Christopher's mind the longer he focused it.

Anne was one of his servants, and he would be damned to catch Owen fucking her.

Christopher straightened at the thought. He never indulged enough to allow these ruminations to bother him to such an extent.

"Do you require anything else, my lord?" Anne asked, breaking him from his darkening thoughts.

"Yes, Anne." He adjusted his cravat. "I have secured a private box to attend a new play this evening at St. James. I would be honored if you would accompany me."

Anne stared at him, her lips parting before she closed her mouth. Her eyes sparkled and a smile broke upon her lips. "I would be delighted." She bowed.

"It is settled then." Christopher retreated to his desk and sat. "You may return to your duties, Anne."

With a nod, Anne left him alone in his study. Once she closed the door, he exhaled and laid his forehead on the desk.

Am I mad? Have I lost all sense of reason? He refrained from knocking his head against the hard surface.

He abhorred the theatre. In fact, he detested all social engagements. The only social fare he tolerated was his club and the den. Those two places became an integral part of his routine thanks to Owen. Even at that moment, his stomach roiled at the thought of attending the ball in a few days but adding the venture to the theatre sent a chill straight through him. He enjoyed a good play as much as the next person, but it involved social interaction, which frankly, he could do without.

The look of pure joy on Anne's face when he invited her to join him had been worth the agonizing paralysis that threatened him at the thought of attending such a function. Why he would put himself out in such a way baffled him. Her smile gave him a gentle reminder.

Because you enjoy her company, you dolt. You long to see her happy, his mind whispered. Such an attachment could prove disastrous. Not only because he was a lord and she a servant in his home, but because the desire building inside of him would inevitably lead to the one thing he was not willing to share with her.

Christopher pulled his journal close and opened the folio of notes. He spent the next several hours buried in his work, studying the research he did with Alistair. If anything, he wished to discover some clue as to what Alistair had done with his metal. It could not have survived the fire, and yet, he knew from their work that the metal did as it wished. Strange as that sounded.

Extreme heat such as exposure to fire and freezing temperatures never altered its form the same way twice. Electricity, as he well knew, was amplified by the metal, and yet it proved too powerful to be attempted a second time. It was almost as if the metal existed as a sentient being, adapting to its surroundings.

Christopher shook his head. Such thoughts were ludicrous. He shoved away the papers on his desk.

As if summoned, Otis' bell sounded and his doors slid open revealing a tray laden with sandwiches and an assortment of cakes, as well as tea.

The aroma lured Christopher close. "As always, you have impeccable timing, Otis."

The dumbwaiter chirped in response.

"Sometimes I wonder if you understand what is being said or if you have a faulty cog somewhere in your circuit system." Christopher removed the tray and carried it to his desk.

Otis beeped twice before closing his doors.

The scent of tea and freshly baked cake filled his study. Christopher could have expired from pure delight. Since he hired Margaret as his cook and housekeeper, he found her to be invaluable. Jameson as well. In fact, hiring Alistair's servants proved to be the wisest thing he had done in a very long time. They were beyond efficient.

Christopher hated the knowledge that his colleague and his family suffered such a fate for him to find a state of comfort. But was that not why he pursued the truth? To assuage some of the guilt that daily haunted his mind to the point of madness.

Work in the laboratory consumed him, feeding his

obsession. Without such, the allure of the den called to him. He sighed before sipping the tea.

He craved answers. *As well as Anne.* He shook his head from the intruding thought of her.

Christopher glanced at the clock. There were still several hours before the play, perhaps a venture out would clear his head.

Once he finished his luncheon, Christopher placed the tray back in Otis' compartment and pressed the button for the kitchen. With a series of beeps and chirps, Otis closed his doors and descended.

Putting away his papers, he noticed a small emblem on the corner of one of the pages. A circle with a rose centered within. He read the notes on the paper and shrugged. Nothing tied the small sketch to the work. He chuckled.

Alistair had small drawings interwoven through his notebooks. Nothing to do with the actual work really, more like the scribbles of an impatient mind. Geometric shapes for the most part, although he noted a few trees sprouting from the corners of the pages on occasion.

Christopher tucked the papers into the folio with a sad smile. He missed his colleague and friend. Together they were on the cutting edge with their work on his mysterious metal. But now all that remained were scribbled notes and a pile of ash.

Before the melancholy could take hold, Christopher tucked the work into one of the drawers and left his study. Perhaps a walk through the park would clear his mind.

Chapter Nine

Jameson entered the kitchen carrying an oversized package. He laid it on the table, causing Margaret to throw up her hands in frustration.

"What in creation do you think you are doing?" She thrust her open hand at the package. "And what is this doing on my table?"

His gaze landed on Adele who stood at the opposite end of the table. "The master said this is for you, Anne, for this evening."

"For me?" Adele asked with a tingling excitement. "What is it?"

"A gown to wear to the theatre, I believe." Jameson bright eyes behind his stoic expression belied his joy for her. He cracked a small smile when he saw her reaction. "Lord Dorrington has instructed that Elizabeth help prepare you for the evening's festivities."

When Lord Dorrington invited her to attend the play that evening, she had been beyond ecstatic. Adele reached for the box and lifted the lid, revealing a deep blue satin gown. Her heart pounded with delight.

"Well then, you better go clean up," Margaret said as she glanced at the box then at Adele. "Jameson and I can handle things around here."

"Go on then, girls," Jameson said with a wave of his hand.

Adele gathered the box in her arms and joined her grinning friend at the servant's staircase. Together they escaped to their shared bedchamber on the top floor.

She threw off the packaging and laid the gown on the bed along with the rest of the undergarments and accessories needed to complete the ensemble. Her fingers traced along the lace edging of the skirt.

"This gown is going to look so lovely," Elizabeth said with a heavy sigh. "Oh, how exciting."

The flurry of activity brought Adele back to her former life. Even though she never had a proper introduction into society, she remembered the process of preparing for an evening of entertainment well. Such a commotion.

Elizabeth styled her hair and applied a small amount of powder, rouge, and lip color. Then came the gown. It fit her to perfection, hugging her curves, creating an elegant silhouette. Not the latest style, to be sure, but Adele could not bring herself to care. The gown was finer than anything she had ever worn.

She pushed away the maudlin thoughts and focused on the evening that lay before her. When she turned to face Elizabeth, emotion choked her.

"You look so beautiful, Anne," her friend said with a smile.

"Do you think this will suit?" Adele asked, turning in a circle.

Elizabeth nodded. "Lord Dorrington will be speechless, mark my words." She handed Adele the white opera gloves, a fan, and a small reticule.

Adele took her friend's hand in her own and held it tight. "Thank you."

"Go, enjoy your evening. Tell me all about it when you return." Elizabeth shooed her out the door. "I shall tell Jameson you are ready."

Elizabeth crossed to the copper communication tube and pressed a button.

Adele barely heard her speak as she stepped out into the hallway. Careful not to trip on her skirts, she descended the main staircase with grace, willing herself not to fall or tear her gown. Once she reached the second-floor landing, she took a deep breath.

Lord Dorrington waited at the bottom of the stairs near the front door with his back to her. A nervous flutter in her stomach made her pause. Would he approve of her appearance?

She descended, watching him.

He turned and spotted her. A look of surprise crossed his face before a darker expression shadowed his features.

Adele hesitated for a moment before pushing forward.

Once she reached his side, he spoke. "You look beautiful this evening."

She acknowledged his compliment with a tilt of her head and a soft smile. Silence stretched between them for the space of a few breaths.

"Will no one question who I am?" she asked.

He tore his gaze from her and cleared his throat. "They may speculate all they wish. Tonight, you are a guest at the theatre. We shall not linger to socialize."

Adele nodded even though a sense of dread settled in the pit of her stomach. The ball was to be her formal appearance as Miss Prescott. This sojourn to the theatre was on a whim.

"Use your fan to mask your appearance, if you are concerned." Lord Dorrington offered his arm. "However, I doubt anyone will even notice our presence."

"And why is that?" she asked.

"There will be plenty of other guests to draw their attention," he said with a half-smile. "I have been informed the Duke and Duchess of Kent as well as the Danish royal family will be in attendance tonight."

With such prestigious guests, they would go unnoticed. She exhaled in relief.

He led her from the house to the brougham parked outside. Andrew held the door for them. His gaze settled on her for a moment before he bowed his head.

Once they settled in the carriage, Adele glanced out the window. Excitement thrummed through her creating a cacophony of emotion deep inside.

When they arrived at St. James' Theatre, she stared up at the building in awe. She drew her fan up to conceal her face from the crowd as they entered the theatre.

Lord Dorrington led her through the milling guests toward the staircase leading to their private box. It seemed as though all eyes remained occupied in locating the more prestigious guests, allowing them to pass unseen. She smiled to herself.

Upon reaching their box, Lord Dorrington offered the seat on the right, providing her a direct line of sight to the stage. She settled on the velvet chair. Her gaze wandered over the opulent sights of the theatre as well as the guests entering.

He handed her a program after he settled into the chair beside her.

The Importance of Being Earnest graced the front cover in floral script. She scanned the program in curiosity. Delight filled her when she realized it was to be a comedy of sorts. Her mood bolstered at the prospect.

She placed the program in her lap and fanned herself. Adele glanced at Lord Dorrington, who seemed engrossed in reading the paper in his hands. The hem of her skirt brushed his trousers. His proximity both unnerved her and brought an odd form of comfort. Her heart fluttered when he glanced up at her.

"Is something troubling you, my lady?" he asked, leaning a bit closer to make his words clear over the noise of the crowd below.

Adele could scarcely trust her voice. "No."

Her gaze refocused on the other theatre guests. Then she noticed a familiar face in the box across the hall. Her uncle. Adele held the fan up, blocking him from her vision.

Lord Dorrington noticed her agitation and followed her gaze. His eyes narrowed.

Before either of them could speak, the lights dimmed signaling the beginning of the play.

Adele watched with rapt attention, but deep in the pit of

her stomach, worry sat like a loadstone.

The play continued unheard as Christopher attuned to his companion's reactions. His gaze flitted back and forth between the stage and Anne.

A wisp of a curl brushed the edge of her scarred jaw. He longed to feel its softness between his fingertips, to savor the scent of her as he drew her close.

Christopher turned his attention back to the stage. His mind, however, remained on the woman beside him. When he saw her descend the staircase earlier, his whole body revolted against his better judgment. She had always been a fetching girl but seeing her in such finery with her head held high set his desire aflame from a controllable smolder. There could be no denying she would very easily pass for Adele Prescott in the right company.

What concerned him at that moment was how much he wanted to cross not only the line of propriety, but the self-imposed isolation that ensured his own safety. Carrying around one's own pain seemed enough of a burden but reaching into the dark recesses of someone's mind and touching their agony compounded with the intense physical consequences of such an action horrified him. As much as he longed for the sensation of her skin beneath his touch, he could not risk such a dangerous desire from ruining both of them.

Anne laughed along with the crowd at something the actor said. Christopher watched her from the corner of his eye. The sweet tilt of her lips and the obvious joy shining in her eyes confirmed the evening had not been wasted.

Christopher glanced down into the crowd and along the row of private boxes lining the theatre. As he suspected, while the crowd's attention focused on the production, they took notice of no one save the prestigious guests in their glittering boxes and the performance. He allowed himself a small smile until his gaze landed on the one man Christopher hoped would not be in attendance that evening. Lord Longmont.

Frantic, he searched to see if Owen joined his father at the theatre. After his friend encountered Anne, Christopher made it clear he wished for her to avoid Owen's presence in the future. Having his friend there would have complicated matters since he would have sought them out, and in doing so, he would have been obliged to introduce her prematurely.

Damn and blast, he cursed himself for a fool. In his attempt to please Anne, he forgot how damned complicated such an event could be. Perhaps he could convince her to leave before intermission to avoid any unwanted social interaction.

He glanced at his companion. She sat entranced by the performers on the stage.

Christopher exhaled in frustration. He could not ask her to leave early. Crushing her joy would make him feel even more of a cad.

His gaze fixed on Longmont once more, who seemed to be more interested in conversation with the man beside him than the play itself. Such behavior would never be tolerated by other guests, and yet he continued in what seemed to be a heated debate with the other man.

When the man left Longmont's booth, Christopher was able to see his face. Mr. Leon Musgrave had been a colleague who aided Alistair and himself in several experiments. During the experiments with the unusual metal, he noted the possibility of such a curiosity being used to manufacture ships or weapons for the military. When the accident occurred, Musgrave cut all ties with the project and deemed the metal unsafe for experimentation. He wished for it to be destroyed, for fear it would fall into the wrong hands.

A wave of curious unease swept through Christopher. What if Longmont used Musgrave to obtain information that would lead to Alistair's death? The possibilities shocked him.

How had he not thought to seek out Musgrave after the fire?

The last words Musgrave spoke to him and Alistair had been in warning of such a powerful material. Musgrave was not a vengeful man, merely a consummate scientist. Of that he could be one hundred percent positive. But why would he aid Longmont?

Such an accumulation of information consumed his thoughts. It was not until Anne laid her hand on his that he realized the intermission began.

Her warmth seeped through his glove. Unbidden, the desire rose again. He met her concerned gaze.

"Are you well, my lord?" she asked.

"I am," he said with a nod. "Are you enjoying the play?"

"Very much so," she replied. Her complexion glowed and her eyes shone bright.

He caught glimpses of this woman beneath the proper maid's attire, and even then, it stirred something to life inside him.

"Thank you for treating me to such a lovely evening." Anne dropped her gaze.

"Think of it as a reward for your hard work." Christopher glanced past her to Longmont's box. He sat staring at them both. The angle of the box and Anne's chair made it impossible for him to see her clearly.

Christopher inclined his head in greeting. Deep inside, panic gripped him. *Damn it all to bloody hell.*

"Come with me, and keep your fan up," he said, taking her hand.

Together, they made their way down the back staircase. Once they reached the lobby, Christopher kept her close as they wove through the guests toward the exit. Breathless, they spilled out into the night air. Without hesitation, Anne took his arm and they walked for a block or two before hailing a hansom cab.

Once they were ensconced in the carriage and moving, Christopher allowed his racing heart to calm. He turned to

Anne.

"I must apologize for my hasty actions," he said.

"No need to apologize, my lord," she assured him. "Lord Longmont is the reason for our hasty retreat, I presume?"

"Yes." He fixed his lopsided top hat. "Unfortunately, it looked as though Lord Longmont wished to have a few words with me, which would have made introductions quite awkward." Christopher caught her smiling. "Something amuses you?" he asked with a huff.

"I do not believe I have seen your composure quite so ruffled, my lord."

"I do not like social gatherings to begin with." He flexed his prosthetic hand. "Lord Longmont is the last person with whom I have any wish to speak."

"Why are you so keen on attending the ball with Miss Prescott if you find such events distasteful?" she asked. "There must be another way we can draw out the culprits."

"The ball is to take place in less than a week." He shook his head. "No, we must proceed as planned."

"If that is your wish." She turned her attention to the window to her left.

"I regret stealing you away from the show this evening, Anne," he said in quiet reflection. "I could see you were enjoying the production."

"I was." Anne exhaled with a soft sigh. "But I understand."

"I promise I shall make it up to you," he vowed.

Anne did not reply, but she did soften her posture, allowing their shoulders to brush in the close confines of the carriage. Christopher forced himself to refrain. He longed to reach for her. Drag her across his lap and kiss her. Awake some passion he knew lived just below her proper façade. Lady or servant, Anne drove him mad.

Once they reached the steps of his townhome, he escorted her to the door and left her there with a murmured goodnight before returning to the carriage and retreating to the club to find Owen. After such an evening, he required some blissful oblivion to drive the lust from his mind.

Chapter Ten

Adele yawned behind her hand as she helped Margaret in the kitchen. She barely slept the night before thanks to her evening with Lord Dorrington. Her mind spent most of the night spinning over the events at the theatre, not to mention the play itself.

While she had been put out by not being able to observe the second half of the production, she understood why Lord Dorrington chose to leave when he did. Disappointment settled in the pit of her stomach on the carriage ride home, only to be compounded when he left her on the steps of his townhouse and ventured off into the night alone.

She never envied a man's freedoms the way she did at that moment. The line she walked grew thinner with every passing day, blurring the reality of her life. Was she a maid? Was she a lady?

The more time she spent with Lord Dorrington, the more she longed for her old life as Miss Adele Prescott. However, living as Anne opened her mind and her eyes to the world so often beyond her purview.

She cut the dough and placed the slices on the tray to be baked. Lost in her own thoughts, she did not hear Jameson approach until he cleared his throat beside her.

"Lord Dorrington has requested your presence in the parlor, Anne," he said.

"Another lesson." She sighed dusting her hands on her apron and then removing the garment. "What is it today, Jameson? Introductions? Conversational etiquette?"

"Dancing, I believe." His lips quirked up in an amused smile. "One of your favorites, if I am not mistaken."

Adele could not stop the smile from gracing her lips.

Dancing had always been one of her favorite activities, second to reading. As she ascended the stairs, a small bounce in her step lightened her heart. He wished to teach her to dance, did he? Well, he would be surprised how quickly she learned. In fact, he might learn a few things from her during this lesson.

The thought of being his dance partner created flutters of excitement in her chest. She wished for nothing more than to lose herself in the music, in the movements.

She entered the parlor and noted all the furniture had been arranged to give them adequate space to dance.

Lord Dorrington stood before a Victrola, arranging a disk on the machine.

"You summoned me, my lord?" she asked by way of announcing her presence.

He glanced over his shoulder. "Yes, I believe there are a few more details we must practice before the ball." He lowered the arm of the machine and the room filled with sweet, familiar music.

Almost without prompting, Adele felt her body begin to sway with the melody. A waltz. How delightful. She caught herself before he turned around.

When he did, he approached her. "Have you ever danced before, Anne?"

"Once or twice," she lied.

He offered his hand in invitation. "Would you care to dance?"

"Nothing would delight me more," she replied with a demure nod and took his hand.

Lord Dorrington drew her into his arms. Their bodies aligned perfectly creating a balance between them. She drew her stance tight, keeping her arms solid, her left hand pressed against his shoulder while her other lay clasped in his.

The heat rose between them as he led her into the dance. He took his time, attempting to guide her in the basic motions. Alas, her body would not be denied as the music infused with her soul. The lessons she savored so long ago came back with a simple turn on the dance floor.

Adele closed her eyes, allowing him to lead, but also allowing the steps to arise from her memories. She savored the music and the dance. With every pass, she found her heart growing lighter as well as her steps.

"I believe you lied to me, Anne." Lord Dorrington's voice interrupted her moment of bliss.

Her eyes snapped open, meeting his curious yet pointed expression. "Whatever do you mean?"

"You dance better than I do," he said with a lopsided smile. "How many times have you waltzed before?" His gaze dropped to her lips, then back again to her eyes.

"A few," she admitted in part. Truth be told, the waltz had always been her favorite dance to practice, even if she never had the opportunity to dance in a social setting before.

Together, they continued the dance, but the lesson became lost along the way. With their bodies moving to the music, their gazes fused, Anne realized how much she enjoyed this moment. She committed every detail to memory. Her first true waltz, and with Lord Dorrington.

Adele marveled at how far she had come. From distrusting to disinterested to disarmed. Lord Dorrington enlightened her to a great many things it seemed.

His grip tightened on her waist as they spun faster, attempting to match the tempo in perfect synchronization. Everywhere his body pressed against hers heated with a delicious friction. She longed to lean against him fully, to feel his warmth seep into her.

Her gaze dropped to his mouth. The softness of his lips contrasted with the sharp angles of his face. Lord Dorrington, with all his dark, brooding features and isolated eccentricities, cut a fine and quite handsome gentleman.

"Why have you not married?" Adele asked, regretting the question as it fell from her lips.

A pang of sadness pierced his eyes before he replied. "Marriage requires intimacy." He paused. "Who would want a broken man?"

"I believe we are all broken in some way," Adele responded, her voice gentle.

He glanced away for a moment before meeting her gaze with his own. Lord Dorrington smiled.

Adele quelled the nervous flutter in her stomach. Lord have mercy, but her heart could not take the ache any longer. Why did he affect her so?

His grip on her waist tightened, drawing her closer. Their steps slowed until it became a calm sway in the midst of the storm of attraction brewing between them.

"You are a strange little bird," Lord Dorrington said in awe. "Somehow I feel a connection to you in ways I cannot comprehend. You quite baffle me."

"Your compliment leaves me speechless." She batted her lashes and smiled.

He spun her, shaking the simpering debutante from her display. He leaned close, his lips nearly brushing her ear. "You are far too clever to play coy, Anne."

Saints above, she would have melted or run from the room, but his arms held her fast. Every fiber of her being protested and craved his proximity, his touch. Adele dared hope for more, even though her rational mind told her to push him away.

She pulled back enough to gaze into his eyes, dark and deep like the sea at midnight. How she longed to brush the wayward lock of hair back away from his face. His handsome face betrayed his desire, and yet she saw the hesitation in every breath he took.

He could have stolen her soul in that instant, and she would have relinquished it without a single solitary regret. Adele dared not speak for fear of shattering the fragile sacred moment.

Damn, hell, and blast! Christopher cursed himself.

Nestled against him, she fit perfectly. Every curve conformed to his body. He wanted so much more than she could imagine. Even though he knew it could never be, having her in his arms, warm and willing and staring up at him with those wide, innocent yet inviting eyes, he felt as though it were possible.

Her lips parted as they swayed to the music. A healthy pink color infused her cheeks, drawing upon her natural beauty. Would she taste as refreshing as she looked, breathless and glowing like a morning sunrise?

The fleeting thought brought Christopher to a realization that scared the devil out of him. Dare he break his rules? Dare he tempt fate and invite such torment on himself for one fleeting touch?

He held his breath. Then he realized she was speaking.

"The music has stopped, my lord," Anne said, and yet she swayed with him to the silence filling the room.

Christopher shook himself from the dangerous direction of his thoughts and stepped away, releasing her from his embrace. She smoothed her skirt and glanced at the Victrola.

He crossed the room and replaced the arm in the cradle, effectively ending the moment. After taking a few breaths to steady his rampaging heart, he turned back to find her a few inches away staring at the music box.

"What a lovely contraption." She touched the edge of the case with her bare fingers. Her gaze focused on him. "Oh, your cravat."

Before he realized what she intended, Anne reached up and tugged his cravat back into place. She smoothed the fabric and her fingertips brushed the skin of his neck.

Christopher braced himself for the onslaught of pain and the rush of her thoughts and memories flooding his mind.

But it never came.

He stared at her in awe.

"My apologies, my lord. I overstepped." She dropped

her hands.

How could that be possible? Even the slightest touch triggered the reaction, and yet Anne's innocent action brought nothing he expected besides the obvious desire for her to touch him again.

"Anne." He reached out his hands. "Remove my gloves."

She hesitated for a second before she tugged the gloves from his hands.

He inhaled at the action. He never allowed himself to be without protection when in the presence of another person. The simple request took on an almost reverent and sensual connotation. Christopher held his breath.

Anne observed him. Her eyes darkened. She twisted his gloves in her hands.

He cupped her chin with his prosthetic hand, and she smiled at him. When he lifted his other, now bare, hand to her cheek, her eyes drifted closed and a soft moan escaped her lips.

No rush of emotion or memory. No agonizing pain seared through his body. Only the simmering need between them and the steady racing of his heart as it should be. Such a simple act of contact, skin to skin, and it nearly brought him to his knees with relief and joy.

He exhaled the breath he had been holding. "How is this possible?" he whispered the question to himself.

Anne rested her hand on his where it lay against her cheek. "You seem surprised."

Christopher laughed. "Oh, my sweet Anne, you delightful creature." He wished he could explain it to her. And yet, so many questions raced through his mind. Could it be possible he had somehow been cured?

"I must go," he said, dropping his hands.

Her countenance shifted. His warm, willing, sweet Anne straightened at the absence of his touch. She handed him his gloves.

"My lord," she said with a forced bow before she

disappeared from the room.

Christopher longed to reach for her, to draw her back into his embrace and kiss her delicious mouth. He shook his head. *No, not yet,* he chided himself. *First you must talk to Musgrave. Tell him what happened.*

Bound and determined to understand what just transpired, Christopher left his townhouse in a rush, hailing a cab to take him to the one man who knew what happened the night Christopher's life changed indefinitely.

Chapter Eleven

Adele retreated up the servant's stairs to her room on the top floor. After reaching the safety of her quarters, she closed the door behind her, leaning her weight against it. Every breath came on short pants, her heart knocking against her chest as though trying in vain to escape.

Waltzing with Lord Dorrington had been one of the single most enjoyable moments in her life. She pressed her hands to her chest. Part of her knew she went too far when she straightened his cravat, but when the tips of her fingers brushed the soft skin of his neck, her need for him burned bright and hot.

How could one innocent touch invoke such a deep-seated desire to come blazing to life? The feel of him warmed her to an uncomfortable level. Even the pendant lying against her heart burned her skin with the radiating heat. She reached inside her blouse and took the pendant in her fist. It warmed and pulsed beneath her touch.

She frowned and inspected her chest where the metal lay against her skin. A red outline marked her skin where the pendant had been, and yet it caused no discomfort, no pain at all. She lifted the pendant to the light from the window and inspected it. The copper color glinted in the midday light, highlighting the circle with the delicate rose in the center.

The racing of her heart slowed as the sadness wove its way back into her thoughts. How she missed her family. Would her father have thought less of her for hiding, lying, and pretending to be someone she was not? Would he have found her burgeoning affection for Lord Dorrington acceptable?

Her father and Lord Dorrington worked side by side for

several years, and yet she never saw him as anything other than her father's scientific partner. Adele often envied the time her father spent on his experimentations, wishing he would have included her somehow.

Lord Dorrington had always been an enigma to Adele. His silent ways and reserved nature bespoke of a man who wished to remain hidden from the world. But what did she know of him in the present aside from his affinity for science and his friendship with her cousin, Owen?

Her eyes fluttered closed at the memory of his strong body pressed to hers as they spun around the dance floor to the sweet, melodic strains of the waltz. His scent still lingered in her memory, enticing a physical response. Her breath quickened, her body swayed, and most of all, she longed for his touch. More than that, she desired to feel the press of his mouth against hers.

Adele craved his kiss. Even though she never experienced one before, it seemed like the only natural progression. Her body directed her mind, repeating the desire again and again until Adele thought her mind would catch fire from the friction and chaos of the thoughts swirling inside.

How could she continue with this charade? She stepped away from the door and sat on the edge of the bed. Lord Dorrington would discover the truth, but how could she continue such a deception? Deep in her heart, she knew the truth should come from her own lips. Lord Dorrington deserved that much.

But what if he should choose to push her away? A heavy ache settled in her chest at the thought.

Even though she agreed to attend the ball and demanded he provide her with a house away from London, away from all who would dare challenge her, the thought of leaving terrified her. She wished at one point to live in anonymity, to disappear forever from society thinking it would be the only way to gain her independence. The very thought of such a life now filled her with dread and sadness.

The door opened.

"Anne, are you well?" Elizabeth asked as she entered the room.

Adele glanced up at her friend and noted the concern in her dark eyes. "Yes, I am. It seems the dancing must have exerted me more than I remembered."

"You should come down to the kitchen. Margaret will be sure to have something to set you to rights again." She smiled with concern.

After adjusting the pendant inside her blouse again, Adele stood and followed Elizabeth from the room. As they descended the stairs in silence, she realized the truth of what she must do.

Upon reaching the kitchen, Margaret fixed a small glass of warm milk for Adele at Elizabeth's insistence. "I can scrounge up a bit of something to settle your stomach, if that will help, my dear." Margaret bustled around her like a flustered mother hen. "You still look a bit warm."

"I assure you, I am well," Adele insisted. She set the glass aside and searched the concerned faces of Elizabeth and Margaret. Jameson entered the room and hovered in the corner with his searching, attentive gaze.

The only person missing from their small group was Andrew, who spent a majority of his time in the stables.

Adele sighed. "I must tell Lord Dorrington the truth."

A visible look of relief passed over her companion's faces.

Elizabeth collapsed on the bench next to her. "Oh, thank heaven for that."

Adele stared at her in surprise. Her gaze shifted to Margaret, whose smile widened.

"I hoped you would come to your senses and tell him." Margaret wrung the towel in her hands. "He is a decent man and will understand when you explain the circumstances to him, dearie."

"We shall support your decision," Jameson added from his corner of the room.

"Is he in his study, Jameson?" Adele asked her body humming with excitement.

"Lord Dorrington has gone out with no instructions as to when he will return."

Adele stood. "Would you please inform me when he returns?"

"Of course, miss," he replied with the hint of a smile.

"Well then, no use in sitting around." Margaret took up her rolling pin. "Back to work, everyone."

Elizabeth grinned as she took Adele by the hand and pulled her toward the stairs. Together they ascended to the parlor on the second floor to put the room back to rights after the dance lesson.

The fresh memories assailed her when she stepped into the room. His scent, his warmth, his piercing stare, and the dark, hungry look in his eyes when she dared cross the line of propriety.

"Anne." Elizabeth turned toward her.

"Yes?" Adele asked when her friend stared at her.

"He kissed you." Elizabeth's eyes widened.

"No." Adele shook her head. "Of course, he did not kiss me. What makes you say such a thing?"

"The look in your eyes when you —" Elizabeth covered her mouth with one hand. "You are taken with him. That must be it."

Adele's heart pounded. What an absurd observation. How could she be in love with a man she hardly knew? "Do not be ridiculous, Elizabeth. How can I love a man I know so little about?"

"Deny it all you wish, but I have seen such dazed expressions before in women who have amorous thoughts toward a certain gentleman." Elizabeth smiled. "I may not be much older than you, but I have seen a great many things in my short life. A servant always does, you know."

"You have gone mad. Did you know that?" Adele ignored her friend's stare as she busied herself with rearranging the furniture.

"Why are you so keen on revealing your true identity then?" Elizabeth asked from behind her.

"I hid to protect myself. We had every reason to believe that my family's deaths were not accidental. Hiding my survival ensured I would live to see the true culprit revealed." Adele forced herself to focus on the task at hand and not turn to face her companion.

"You once believed Lord Dorrington to be this culprit," Elizabeth observed.

"I did." She straightened the chair by the window.

"And now you wish to reveal your secret to him?"

"I am to reveal it to the whole of London at the ball."

"But under the guise of a deception. Pretending to be a maid who agreed to pretend to be a lady who hid her survival from family and friends." Elizabeth rounded on her, meeting her gaze. "And you think I am the one who has gone mad?"

"What else am I to do?" Adele asked in frustration. "I must tell him before the ball. It is the only way I can go through with it. He must know the truth."

"I agree." Elizabeth took her hand. "And we will support you. But I must know, do you love him?"

"Honestly, I do not know." She sighed.

"You desire him." Elizabeth smiled. "There is no denying that."

"I cannot deny it," Adele replied.

"Then you must tell him the truth this evening." Elizabeth dropped her hand and returned to tiding the room.

But what if he does not desire me? Adele asked herself as she finished arranging the pillows. The memory of Lord Dorrington's quick dismissal stung. He could have kissed her, but why did he push her away instead?

Christopher pulled his hat a bit lower as he approached the row of homes where Musgrave resided. It was not as fashionable as the area where he lived, but the homes were well maintained and visually pleasing.

His mind flashed back to the instant Anne touched him. He could still feel the warmth of her hand, and yet the shock overwhelmed him that he forgot the bliss of such a simple, yet erotic action. Where pain should have been, only the pleasure prevailed.

The possibility remained constant. He could have somehow been cured of his affliction. And yet, he feared the reality of having to test this theory with another willing person. Which led him to Musgrave.

In truth, seeing Musgrave at the theatre prompted the reason for the visit, but Anne's innocent touch compounded his reasoning for the necessity of it.

Two men knew of his affliction, and one of them had the unfortunate fate of encountering it firsthand. Christopher knew Musgrave's deepest thoughts, his memories, his desires, his misfortunes, and they came at the cost of immense pain and a week's recovery in bed. After the incident, Christopher vowed never to touch another living soul skin to skin for fear of reliving such a harrowing experience.

If anyone could help him, Musgrave could.

Upon locating the correct number, Christopher ascended the steps to Musgrave's home. He knocked several times and waited, tapping his fingers against his cane. After several moments passed, Christopher knocked again. Still there was no reply.

He tried the knob, which turned under his hand, allowing him admission into the house. Christopher closed the door behind him and noticed the absence of any servants.

"Good day, is anyone home?" he called out, setting his

hat and cane aside on the table by the entrance.

When no one replied, Christopher looked in the drawing room. As he drew the door open, he noticed the figure lying on the floor next to the fireplace. His once friend and scientific ally lay on the floor, face down in a pool of blood. Musgrave was dead.

Christopher dropped to his knees beside the body knowing his friend was already gone. He noted the large gash in the back of Musgrave's head. Blood and hair matted the wound. He turned his head in an effort to keep down his lunch.

With a trembling hand, Christopher removed his glove and laid his bare fingers against Musgrave's neck. The body remained warm, and yet he felt nothing. No spark of life, no flash of memories, just an empty void. He sighed and collapsed back against the chair a few feet away from the deceased.

He tugged his glove back on.

"Oh, my heavens!" A voice near the door startled him.

Christopher glanced up and saw a man standing over them, horror emblazoned on his face, his hand covering his mouth. He wore simple clothes and carried himself with the air of a man in service.

"Are you one of Musgrave's servants?" Christopher asked, rising from the floor.

"I am, my lord. I am his butler, Maxwell," the man replied before staring at his master, his face pale and hands trembling. "What has happened here, my lord?"

"I came in and found him like this." Christopher made his way around the room. "Where were you?"

"Mr. Musgrave sent me on an errand just after he received a visitor this morning, my lord."

Christopher spun to face the butler. "Did this visitor present a card?"

"Yes, my lord." The butler retreated to a silver platter where the calling cards were placed. He picked up the one atop the pile and presented it.

A brief glance confirmed Christopher's suspicion. *Magnus Prescott, the Right Honorable Viscount of Longmont.* Dread coiled in his gut, souring what was left of his afternoon meal.

"How long were you absent?" Christopher asked.

"An hour or so, my lord."

"And the other servants?" Christopher tucked the card into his pocket.

"Today is their day off, my lord." He turned away from the body, facing Christopher. "Shall I fetch the constable, my lord?"

"Yes, please do so."

The butler bowed and retreated from the room, a look of obvious distress on his face. Even the most stalwart of servants would break under such conditions.

Careful not to disturb more than necessary, Christopher walked around the room taking inventory. He noted nothing out of the ordinary for a contemporary gentleman's drawing room. As he approached the window, he glanced back at Musgrave's body. No one would have seen anything from the street considering the density of the curtains in the window. He drew one back allowing light to stream into the room.

A flash of gold on the body caught his attention. He dropped the curtain and proceeded to the spot where he saw the glimmer of metal. Tucked between the victim's fingers lay a small golden object. Christopher removed it and held it in his palm.

A golden cufflink. He turned it over, inspecting the engraving. The Longmont seal.

Christopher swore. Lord Longmont killed Musgrave.

He placed the cufflink in his pocket next to the calling card. A sliver of conscience rose up telling him to turn the evidence over to the authorities. Hesitation lingered as the questions began to form in his mind. Why would Longmont kill Musgrave? Did it have something to do with their experiments with the metal? Could Longmont know the truth behind its power and his subsequent abilities? His head pounded with the unanswered possibilities.

With one last look at the man he had once known, a man who inadvertently shared his life with Christopher in a single thoughtless action of kindness, Christopher took his leave. He gathered his belongings at the door and left the house of death.

Lost in his thoughts, Christopher wandered the city. Up streets he recognized, down others he did not. He fought the desire to confront Longmont. He could not. Not yet. Not with his plans for the ball and the event being so close. He would wait, certain an opportunity would produce itself.

The sun disappeared beyond the horizon, giving way to the darkness. Christopher avoided his club even though his stomach growled with hunger. His mind raced, and he turned away from the street that would lead him to the Floating Den and blissful oblivion. He craved it, and even so, he knew beyond a doubt that a clear head would be required for the next steps in his plan.

Exhausted and frustrated, Christopher ambled toward home.

"My lord, welcome home." Jameson's greeting cheered him as he stepped into the warm, familiar surroundings.

"Have Otis deliver supper to my study if you will, Jameson." He passed his hat and cane to the butler.

"As you wish, my lord." Jameson left him, heading toward the kitchen.

Christopher ascended the stairs. He opened the door to his study and sighed in relief at the comfort of his own solitude.

The decanter of whisky sat glimmering in the firelight. He crossed the room and poured a glass. When he turned, he realized he was not alone. He stopped short, studying the woman sitting by the fireplace with a book in her lap.

"Anne, what in the blazes are you doing in my study at

this hour?" He set the glass aside.

"I needed to speak with you," she said dropping her gaze to the book before closing it and standing.

Christopher braced himself as she approached him. The events of the day weighed heavy on his mind, but her presence brought a sweet air of relief. He wanted her, by God. He wanted her more than anything on God's green Earth. But he still possessed an ounce of propriety toward her, lady or not.

She stopped beside him and took the glass from his hand. He watched, stunned as she brought it to her lips and drank. Heat and desire infused him.

"Why are you here, truly?" he asked, his voice hoarse and his body screaming for her touch.

Anne glanced at him over the rim as she took another drink. This time she finished the liquor and set the glass aside. She poured him another drink and handed him the glass.

Her cheeks glowed rosy in the firelight, warmed by the whisky. His gaze dropped to her lips where they gleamed wet and ripe. He took a drink to stop himself from kissing her then and there. Her actions rendered him immobile, but her words left him speechless.

"I have come to make my confession."

Chapter Twelve

The burn of the whisky lingered on the back of her tongue. What had she been thinking? Her nerves took control and she needed something to fortify her. But standing this close to Lord Dorrington, feeling the warmth of him, inhaling his spicy scent, Adele struggled to calm the racing of her own heart.

He stared down at her, curiosity and hunger in his eyes. Never in her life had a man looked at her in such a manner. It made her body weak and hot, and still it bolstered her courage.

"Confessions?" he said with a small quirk of the lips. "Have you sinned? For I am no priest."

Adele closed her eyes, unable to speak while he teased her in such a way. "I am in earnest, my lord. I must tell you the truth." When she opened her eyes, his expression grew somber.

"Very well then." He gestured to the wing backed chairs situated near the fireplace.

A distance between them granted an air of relief for a moment, allowing Adele to refocus her mind on the conversation. Being in his company had become something of a distraction and that concerned her. Her plans began to crumble the moment she glimpsed his passion in the pursuit of the truth.

She sighed as she sat down.

Lord Dorrington sat relaxed, his leg crossed over the other, his hands resting on the arms of the chair. She could not read his expression, but found his attention bestowed solely on her.

Then she noticed the red on his sleeve.

"Are you injured, my lord?" She stood and reached for his hand. Before he could pull away, she peeled his coat sleeve back to reveal a small blotch of dark blood on his pristine white cuffs.

"Oh, damnation." He jerked his hand away. "I am quite fit." He met her gaze. "It is not my blood."

Adele stepped back, pulling her hands to her chest. Fear rose inside her. "Whose blood is it then?"

Lord Dorrington stood and leaned against the mantle for a moment before turning back to her. "I called upon a friend. Someone who worked with Alistair and myself on some experiments." He paused. "He was dead when I arrived at his home."

She gasped and sat on the chair, her mind spinning. "What was his name?"

"Musgrave."

Her eyes fell closed. She knew Mr. Musgrave since she was a small child. He had always been kind to her. He disappeared a few weeks before her father died. She mourned him as she had her own family.

"What happened?" she asked her voice faint.

"Murder, I suspect." Lord Dorrington turned to face her.

She pressed a hand to her chest, covering the pendant beneath her blouse. "Why would anyone kill such a harmless gentleman?"

"Musgrave worked with Alistair and myself. He would have had an intricate knowledge of our experiments." He pinched the bridge of his nose and shook his head. "Someone wanted information, I believe."

"What could possibly be worth murder?" she asked, horrified.

"You might as well know the whole story since I have embroiled you in this disastrous charade." He sat across from her again, his demeanor shaken. "The material we were examining had very...distinctive properties. It was a fragment of metal, super conductive and sensitive to a vast array of elements."

Adele listened, soaking in the information.

"I believe somehow word spread to those who would use the metal as a weapon of sorts." He seemed to be thinking as he spoke. "I believe that is why the lab was vandalized and why the Prescott family was killed. Someone wanted this material so desperately they were willing to murder to obtain it and its secrets."

"But why kill Musgrave? You said yourself the metal was lost in the fire." Adele tried to fathom the reality of the situation.

"I do not know." Lord Dorrington raked his hand through his hair, mussing it. "Damn and blast," he mumbled beneath his breath. "Perhaps we should not attend the ball after all."

"Why ever not?" Adele feared she already knew the answer to her own question, but she persisted.

"It was never my wish to put you in harm's way." He met her gaze, steady and unwavering. "I fear the appearance of Miss Prescott would cause much more than a scandal, it would put you in grave danger."

His concern for her safety touched her heart. "But if we do not attend, then how shall we draw out the murderer?"

"I cannot—no, I will not—put you in such a position." He glanced into the fire before meeting her eyes again. "It was wrong of me to ask such a thing of you from the very beginning."

Adele remembered her reason for becoming a maid in his house. She willingly put herself in danger to discover the truth. There would be no retreat. "You did not need to ask me for I came of my own volition." She held his gaze. "I came into your service hoping to have the opportunity to discover the truth, and you have presented the perfect plan to uncover the villain behind my family's murder."

Lord Dorrington's brow rose as he leaned forward. "Your family?"

"Yes, my lord," she said, her courage wavering. "My name is not Anne, it is Adele." She paused. "Adele Prescott."

His expression shifted from shock to one of disbelief. When he rose to his feet, Adele fought to remain in her chair, her hands wringing in her lap. She wished to tell him the truth, but fear consumed her. She waited, agonizing over his response. Silence lingered between them, drawn out by the tension.

He stood facing the painting above the fireplace, his hands braced on the mantle.

"How could I have been so blind?" The rhetorical question broke the silence. He turned his eyes clear and dark. "Of course, you are. The similarities, your perfect ability to behave as a lady should in polite society..." He paused, licking his lips. "The way you waltz."

Warmth infused her cheeks at his offhanded compliment. "It was not my intention to deceive you, my lord. I wished only to discover the truth."

"How in God's name did you survive that inferno?" he asked.

"I fell asleep in the library while I was reading," she began, the memories flooding her with pain and sorrow. "When I woke, smoke filled the room. I ran into the hallway, but the upper levels of the house were already ablaze. I tried to climb the stairs, to save my family, but they collapsed and I fell." She hesitated before continuing. "When I woke, Margaret and Jameson were with me. My hands were burned as well as my face, and my whole body ached."

"An angel watched over you that day," he said.

"As time passed, I realized, along with Margaret and Jameson, that the fire had been set intentionally." She turned from him. "I needed to know the truth."

"You believed I had something to do with the fire?" Lord Dorrington asked. No malice laced his words, just curiosity.

Adele nodded. "When you hired all my father's servants, I decided to remain in hiding and work for you. Anne was my ladies' maid and a dear friend. She perished in the fire. I took her name and her position."

"That would explain the animosity I noticed between Andrew and yourself," he said. "He lost his sister the day you lost your family."

"Yes, and I can hardly blame him for it." She blinked back the tears that threatened. "I am a daily reminder of his grief."

Lord Dorrington knelt down and hooked his finger beneath her chin, lifting her face level to his. "Why have you suffered in silence? You must know by now I am loyal to your family. Alistair was one of my closest friends. Part of me died that day. I still blame myself for their horrible fate."

Adele reached up and cupped his face in her hand. His skin warmed her palm. His eyes drifted closed at the intimate action. This time he did not pull away at the contact.

"You need not blame yourself." She stroked his cheek with her thumb. "I know how much you loved my father." Adele sighed. "Before he died, my father gave me a token of his love. He swore it would always protect me. Perhaps the reason I survived is to help you discover the truth." She paused and withdrew the pendant from inside her blouse. "It may be silly, but I keep it close, hoping he watches over me still. It is my last connection to him."

"May I see it?" Christopher asked.

With a nod, she unclasped the pendant and removed it. "Perhaps it will offer you the same comfort it has afforded me." Adele placed the pendant in his hand and closed his fist around it.

Their eyes locked. A moment suspended in time. Her gaze flickered to his lips before returning to his haunting gaze. She smiled before standing.

"Goodnight, my lord," she said before taking her leave.

Adele exited the room, the scent of him clinging to her, the pull of him nearly impossible to ignore. How she wanted to draw him close, kiss his lips, comfort him in the ways she wished to be comforted. Her heart raced as she climbed the stairs toward her bedchamber.

Her heart yearned for him even though distance cooled her ardor. A strange ache settled in her chest, but deep inside, she knew if she remained with him one moment longer she might act on her impulse and cross a very delicate line.

The room stilled with an eerie silence after the door closed behind her. Christopher sat in his study staring at the door with the pendant clenched in his fist. His heart raced, his mind spun. Unanswered questions and desperation clawed at his brain.

Her scent lingered in the room. The haunting reminder of her warm touch burned his skin. He longed to run his fingers through her hair and along the soft column of her neck. More than anything, he wanted to taste her lips, feel the press of them against his own. Damn and blast, but he craved her completely. He shook his head from the lustful thoughts and focused instead on both of their confessions.

Their conversation turned over in his mind again and again. How could he not have seen the truth?

He pushed himself out of the chair and paced the room. Had he not wanted to reveal Miss Prescott to the world at Lord Longmont's ball? Christopher would be a fool to believe providence brought her to his home. No, his plan had been foolhardy at best. His desire to bring an innocent into his dangerous game should have brought shame. Yet it was when she revealed her true identity could he bring himself to find fault with his own plan.

Adele suffered enough. Even though she vowed her assistance no matter the threat, Christopher cringed at the thought of putting her in such a precarious situation. His affection for her ran deeper than he cared to admit.

The pendant warmed in his palm. He opened his fist and

glanced down. The metal glowed and pulsed with a warmth that defied logic. A familiar rush of energy consumed him. *It could not possibly be —*

He lifted the necklace closer, studying the image on the face of the pendant. A delicate rose...a familiar rose. He paused for a moment before rushing to his desk and drawing out the folio containing all of his notes for the experiment that ruined him.

Foreboding and excitement charged through his veins as he leafed through the notes. He stopped when he reached the pages littered with small intricate sketches. Alistair's small additions to the edges of the notes captured his attention. He turned a few more pages before finding the image that confirmed his fear.

A single rose curled up into a perfect blossom in a circle nestled between scribbled words and irregular geometric patterns. Christopher laid the pendant next to the image on the paper. He scoffed in disbelief. The rose was identical.

"You clever man," Christopher mumbled in awe.

After the lab had been found torn apart yet nothing taken, Alistair was convinced the thieves were sent to take the metal. They agreed it would be better to hide their experiment until they found a more secure facility to use. The metal remained in Alistair's possession for safekeeping. He never would have imagined that Alistair would transform it into something so innocuous and beautiful.

Christopher lifted the pendant to the light, admiring the way the copper color absorbed the heat and gleamed like polished silver. The impurities had been stripped from it. All that remained was pure metal.

Alistair gifted it to his daughter knowing it would be well hidden and guarded from those who wished to steal it. A chuckle escaped him. How clever indeed.

He collapsed in his chair, cradling the pendant in his fist. He could not feel the warmth in his mechanical palm, but the energy coursed through him. That familiar ebb and flow of unknown force he felt before when the electrical current coursed through the metal and into him set his body on edge once more.

How could she not have felt it? If she wore it every day since the fire, how was it possible for her to ignore the obvious current that terrified and thrilled him?

Perhaps she could not recognize it. He stared at the innocuous little object tucked between his gloved fingers.

"What a frightful lot of trouble you have caused us all," he murmured to the necklace. "I wish I left you hidden in the desert sand."

"Talking to yourself again?" a voice cut into the blissful silence.

Christopher tucked the pendant into his pocket. "Prescott, I did not hear you knock." He shuffled the papers together and tucked them into the folio.

Owen's gaze skimmed the room as he entered. "Forgive me, old chap, but I was on my way back from the club and wanted to be sure you had not left for the Floating Den without me."

"Ah yes." Christopher cleared his throat. "Well, it was quite a taxing afternoon, so I believe I will be turning in early this evening."

Owen stared at him in mock horror. "Have you taken leave of your senses?"

"It is possible," Christopher mumbled. "My apologies."

"You are still attending my father's ball, are you not?" Owen tugged at his sleeves. "I shall be escorting the fairest lady in all of London. I would hate for you to miss out on the social event of the season."

"Yes, I will be in attendance." Christopher assured him.

"I shall take up no more of your time then," Owen said with a smile. "Unless you have changed your mind and wish to join me at the den."

The desperate part of his mind begged to follow. His body craved the addictive substance. He fought against the urge, instead focusing on the woman who consumed his thoughts.

"I thank you for the invitation, but I must decline." Christopher rose to his feet.

"As you will then," Owen said with a nod before placing his hat back on his head. "Until tomorrow."

Christopher exhaled in relief when his friend left. He placed the papers back in his desk drawer and locked it before tucking the key into his waistcoat pocket.

He glanced at the fire dying in the grate and extinguished the light in his study. As he climbed the staircase, he found his feet taking him past his bedchamber and up the last flight of stairs.

Christopher paused outside the room Anne and Elizabeth shared. He closed his eyes. *Adele.* He opened the door and found both women asleep, the small fire glowing enough to provide warmth and a smidgen of light.

Without a sound, he crossed to where Adele laid, her braid snaking across her pillow, her face peaceful in slumber. He admired her beauty for a moment before removing the pendant from his pocket and placing it on the nightstand beside the bed.

The safest place for it would be where it had been all along. He could not tell her. Not yet.

He removed his gloves and brushed his bare fingers across the soft curve of her jaw.

A jolt of pain surged through him and a flash of images played through his mind. Adele reading in a window seat. Adele playing with her brother. Alistair and his wife. And flames licking the walls, consuming everything it touched.

He jerked his hand away and focused his mind to block out the pain. Perhaps his ability did not disappear as he thought. He stared down at Adele as she shifted in slumber. Her lips parted.

"Christopher," she whispered in her sleep. A smile graced her lips.

His heart clenched as he pulled a glove onto his prosthetic hand. He paused for a movement. Focusing all his mental strength, he reached out and pressed a fingertip to her temple.

His body flinched, but no pain assailed him. He delved through her mind, searching through her memories and thoughts until a familiar face caught his attention. His own. He selected the memory as one would a book from a shelf and opened it as though he were reliving the moment in vivid detail.

Their waltz. His body reacted seeing the moment from her perspective, feeling her emotions as though they were his own. He gasped at the onslaught of confusion, desire, and passion contained in that single memory.

He pulled away, snapping the book closed and removing himself from her mind.

She moaned and rolled away, but never woke.

Christopher fled the room, afraid of what he learned and what he saw that day. He rushed to the safety of his bedchamber and closed the door behind him, shuttering him away from the world.

He longed for blissful abandon and wished for a moment he had joined Owen at the Floating Den. The powerful images he saw in Adele's mind haunted him. They terrified him.

What he discovered could never be ignored. If Christopher unleashed his demons, there would be no way to contain them. His stomach roiled, and he spent the better part of the night physically ill.

Chapter Thirteen

Adele bustled around the kitchen, her heart lighter than it had been in months. At breakfast, she informed the rest of the servants of her confession the evening before. A visible air of relief passed over the small group. Well, except for Andrew, whose surly disposition did nothing to distract from Adele's positive mood.

When she woke, she was surprised to find her father's gift waiting for her on the nightstand. Lord Dorrington must have returned it after she retired. Her dreams had been filled with vivid memories and delicious desires. Even though she felt rested, a hunger rose within her. One she could not fill with food or drink, but only with the presence of Lord Dorrington. Her face heated at the memory of him in her dreams.

Pushing the thoughts aside, she arranged the tray and carried it to Otis.

Jameson stopped her as she pressed the button to call the dumbwaiter. "Lord Dorrington has requested you bring the tray up directly."

Adele blinked before nodding. "Very well."

She carried the tray to Lord Dorrington's study. Upon entering, she spied him reading at his desk. Her heart fluttered at the sight. His hair seemed a bit unkempt and it was clear he had not shaved yet. But he wore a clean, pressed suit and a sharp cream-colored cravat.

He glanced up from his papers and smiled. "Thank you, Anne." He paused. "Would you rather I call you Miss Prescott from now on?"

"Whichever you prefer, my lord." She set the tray on the desk and bowed.

"Come now," he said as he stood. "There is no reason to continue this charade, is there?"

Adele met his inquisitive eyes. "No, my lord."

"Take a walk with me, Miss Prescott." He rounded the desk and motioned for the door.

"But your breakfast?" She glanced at the tray.

"It will be here when I return." He opened the door. "Come."

Adele followed him down the stairs to the front entrance where Jameson waited for them with their outer garments. She tried to read his stoic expression when he aided her with her wrap, but he remained impassive.

She stepped out into the brisk morning air. The clouds hung low in the sky casting a grey hue on the street and the houses. "It looks like rain."

Lord Dorrington paused for her to come alongside him. "I believe it will hold off long enough."

Together they walked in silence. The sounds of the carriages and bustle of city life drowned into the background. Adele could focus only on the man beside her and the thrumming of her own heartbeat. They rounded a corner and walked two more blocks before reaching the park.

Adele moved to enter the park but stopped when Lord Dorrington came up short. "Are we not going into the park?"

He shook his head and continued walking.

Confused, Adele followed him, nearly running into his broad back when he came to a stop. They stood before a modest home with a clear view of the park.

Lord Dorrington stared up at the front of the house.

Adele's gaze vacillated between the house and Lord Dorrington for a moment before she spoke. "Who lives here?" she asked, curiosity overtaking her sense.

"My aunts," he replied.

"They both live here?" Adele glanced at the house again. A simple flowerbox sat in the front window of the well-kept building.

"Yes." He turned to face her. "Aunt Prim is a widow. Has been for almost twenty years. My Aunt Cordelia lives with her. She never married."

His explanation was short, clipped, almost as if it caused him physical pain to speak the words. Adele studied his expression, but she could read nothing of his inner thoughts.

"I am sure they are wonderful," Adele said before almost forgetting herself and asking if they should pay them a visit.

He sighed.

"Why have you brought me here?" Adele studied him.

"Once your true identity is revealed at the ball this evening, you cannot remain in my home as my servant." Pain flickered in his eyes followed by regret. He blinked and composed himself.

"You promised me a home in the country where I could disappear." Her stomach churned at the thought of leaving him at all. She pushed through the disappointment. "That was our bargain."

"Yes, well, that was also struck before I knew the reality of your situation." He took her arm and led her across the street to a bench just inside the park hidden by a row of trees. "Once Longmont speaks with you, he will know you are no imposter."

"That may be so, but I have no intention of remaining in town." She straightened before sitting on the bench. "I shall take my leave come morning."

"Do you not care to see your parents avenged?" he asked, sitting down beside her.

Adele blinked away the tears threatening to overwhelm her. "I realize that nothing I say or do, even if our plan should uncover the identity of the villain who stole my family away, will ever bring them back to me."

"No, it will not bring them back." He spoke in a gentle, understanding tone. "But it may offer you a chance to grieve properly seeing their murderer punished for his crimes." He took her hand in his own. "You must stay and see this through to its conclusion."

"If I stay, my uncle will demand I live with them as they are my closest living relatives." Bile stung the back of her throat. "I would rather disappear without knowing the truth of my parents than live under his roof."

His face darkened. "Why do you think I offered lodging with my aunts? They will understand, and I know you will be safe with them."

"How can you possibly know that?" she asked with a weary sigh.

"Because no one will know where you are," he replied. "I need you close to me if I am to protect you."

She searched his face. Her gaze lingered on his lips before returning to his. "Then do not send me away at all," she whispered.

"You are a lady." He released her hand and stood. "I cannot in good conscience keep you under my roof once London is aware of your miraculous survival."

"So, you will push me away for the sake of my reputation?" She scoffed. Rising from her seat, she threw one last shot before taking her leave. "How noble of you."

The entire walk home, Adele was acutely aware of his presence. He remained a few paces behind like a guardian angel. She did not need protection. Not when her heart was already broken and her reputation in questionable ruins. Once the truth came to light, none of it would matter. She would leave and never return.

As she approached his townhouse, Adele dashed the tears away. She circled around the back of the house to use the servant's entrance.

Inside, she closed the door and leaned against it. Her breathing ragged and her heart pounding, she gathered herself willing the tears to stop. She made her way up the servant's stairs. When she reached the second floor, she stopped.

Lord Dorrington stood waiting for her. "Come with me."

"You do not have the right to demand anything from me," she spat, her anger overtaking any sense of decorum.

He snatched her by the wrist and pulled her through the hall to his study. Once inside, he closed the door and locked it.

Fear, uncertainty, and desire raged through her. The feral expression on his face and the hunger in his eyes made her back away until her legs hit the desk. She wanted him desperately, but she would be damned if she let him know just how much.

Lord Dorrington cornered her, and Adele had no wish to escape.

Adele stared at him, her eyes wide, her mouth parted, breaths quick and uneven. The flush of her cheeks and the shift of her eyes to a deep oceanic blue betrayed her arousal. He leaned against the door and studied her.

"How dare you treat me in this manner." She tipped her chin up, defiance reflecting in her posture.

"In this moment, you are my servant," he said, unable to believe the sternness of his own words. "If you wish to remain under my roof until after the ball, then you will remain as such."

"You just said —"

"I know damned well what I just said," he snapped and ran a hand through his hair. "Confound it, woman. Do you not realize how dangerous this is? Your reputation will be tenuous at the very best once you reveal yourself this evening." He stepped closer. "Will you not heed my advice and remove yourself from me?"

"Why must I do as you bid only to be shuffled off to some other man for him to dictate my worth and where I belong?" She held his gaze. "Is it too much to ask for me to choose my own path?"

"My mind will not be at ease until I am assured of your safety." Christopher reached for her, but she drew away, shaking her head.

"That does not answer my question." She frowned.

Christopher longed to claim her, to put any question of where she belonged to rest. He could easily give her a cottage in the country and mask her in a shroud of anonymity. It would be nothing to whisk her away that very moment and hide her from the world, even from himself. His heart screamed from inside his chest, *No, do not let her go.*

The alternative terrified him.

"Your silence speaks louder than words, my lord." She circled around him toward the door.

He stepped into her path, blocking her.

"Step aside, my lord." She met him bold conviction. "If you will not uphold your end of our agreement, then I shall be on my way."

"Be reasonable, Adele."

She gasped at the sound of her given name on his tongue. He savored the reaction, wanting more from her than just the honor of using her Christian name. More than that, he wished to hear his own on her sinful lips.

"My lord," she said her voice low, her tone serious.

"Christopher," he corrected her.

A crimson hue blossomed across her cheeks. She glanced away. "Please, release me."

"Is that what you truly wish?" he asked. Christopher reached for her hand again. When she allowed him to take her hand in his own, a sense of rightness settled deep in his soul. "You wish to leave everything behind."

"You have given me no alternative I wish to pursue," she replied with a heavy sigh.

His mind warred with his heart, knowing that moment defined the point of no return, and within such a situation, he would find no easy outcome for either of them. "I cannot keep you under my roof. Not as my servant and certainly not as

Miss Prescott."

Even though there was a way to keep her as his own, he could never enslave her to his twisted melancholy. He would not shackle her. Not to a broken man such as himself. Yet the thought of her married to someone else sent a bolt of envy through him like an electrical current.

He pulled her close, catching her unaware. She pressed her flattened palm to his chest. With one arm around her shoulders, he held her tight against him.

"I cannot...I will not fight against it any longer." He caressed her cheek with his fingertips, longing to feel the warmth of her skin. "Try as I might, my flesh is weaker than my resolve. For that I apologize, and yet I cannot beg the forgiveness of my heart for craving you so ardently." He memorized the shape of her face, the depth of her eyes, the plump lines of her lips as they curved in surprise. "Nothing about my actions reflects kindness."

"You have been nothing but gracious to me, my lord," she whispered.

He scoffed. "I have been damned selfish. And may the Lord forgive me for being so, but I want more." He removed his gloves and drew her into his arms again. "You have bewitched every fiber of my being."

Adele's eyes drifted closed as he cradled her face in his hands. He braced himself for the rush of memories and emotions, but they never came. Warmth radiated between them. The heat released the scent of pure need, intoxicating them both. His fingertips delved into the soft strands of hair framing her face.

When she moaned, the last of his reservations slipped away. Christopher kissed her lips with soft reverence, uncertain of his body's reaction to her. The coil of desperation that unraveled shocked him. Heat and need pooled deep in the pit of his stomach then ventured lower, drawing him into a void where nothing existed but the two of them and that intimate moment.

Adele wrapped her fingers around his lapels. Her tongue brushed his lower lip and Christopher lost all sense of rational thought. He parted his lips, inviting her closer with a nudge of his hands. She acquiesced with a sigh. It melted the final vestiges of his restraint.

He tasted her. Every emotion, every hope poured into the kiss. As their tongues danced, Christopher coaxed her deeper into his embrace, his hands roaming over her shoulders, down her back, then up to thread through her silken hair.

Heaven above, he wanted her. With every beat of his heart, every whispered breath, he desired nothing so much as the woman in his arms. All thoughts of the plan, of the murder, of her conniving uncle drifted into a void hidden in the back of his mind. Adele consumed him. Her scent ensnared him, and her kiss seduced him. She bewitched him entirely.

"Christopher," she whispered against his mouth. Her hands framed his face, her palms warm against his skin.

The melody of his name on her lips brought him a stinging bliss as reality once again encroached on their solitary moment. He licked his lips and pulled away in an attempt to cool the ardor between them. His body raged against his mind. *Take her. Claim her. Make her your own.* He shook the thoughts from his lust fogged brain.

"Christopher," she repeated her voice louder yet still laced with awe and breathy with need.

"My apologies," he said, finally able to step away from her. If he held her much longer, he would damage both of their reputations beyond repair. Hers more so.

A brief flash of pain crossed her delicate features when he removed himself from her touch. "And still after such a display of passion, you will push me away?"

"I must," he confessed. "Believe me when I say it pains me more than you can possibly comprehend." His heart ached at the loss of contact and knowing he inflicted the hurt reflected in her eyes.

She nodded once to acknowledge his decision and clasped her hands before her. "I shall take my leave then."

"Do not go, Adele." The words rushed forth from his lips before he could halt them.

"If you do not wish to proceed with our prior arrangement, then I must take my leave." She met his gaze, her resolution mirrored in her weary expression. "I cannot remain in this house. Or in London."

Christopher's heart dropped into the soles of his shoes. He could not, would not let her go. Would he? *Damnation!* He berated himself for the fool he so obviously seemed to be.

When she turned to open the door, Christopher crossed the room and placed a firm hand on the door, holding it closed.

She sighed but did not turn to face him. "Am I to be your prisoner now?"

Desperation clawed at him. He needed to convince her to stay, but pretty words and empty promises would never hold sway over her. He brandished a piece of truth like a shiny bauble meant to entice children and thieves.

"I believe your uncle may be behind your father's death."

The air between them shifted away from desire to something much more visceral. Her whole body stiffened.

"Why would my uncle want my family dead?" Her question lingered between them.

"In all honesty, I have not quite been able to understand his motives." Christopher warred with his conscience to keep from pulling her against him and holding her tight. "Until recently, I could only speculate."

"You have no solid proof of your accusation?" she asked, her hand wrapped around the doorknob.

"To tie him to the fire and your family's deaths, no." He paused. "However, I believe he murdered Musgrave."

Adele gasped and spun to face him. "Why would he harm such a sweet man?"

"Your uncle has harbored an unhealthy desire to obtain the research we compiled on the metal." He removed his hand from door and straightened his waistcoat. "Musgrave had information that would have made your uncle quite persistent in obtaining that metal and all our research."

"But it was all lost in the fire." Adele shook her head in disbelief. "This cannot be true."

"Your uncle has always coveted your father's position as well as his title," Christopher said.

"He made no secret of his desire for my father's inheritance." She shook her head again. "But I cannot believe he would stoop as low as to murder my family to obtain it."

"Lord Longmont is behind it all, mark my words," Christopher vowed, his fervor igniting a passion deep in the pit of his stomach.

"How can you be so sure my uncle has any hand in this devious plot?" She narrowed her gaze in challenge.

"I found one of his cufflinks at Musgrave's home, near his body."

"Show me," she demanded.

Christopher crossed the room and opened the top drawer in his desk. He glanced up to find Adele standing beside him, staring down at the contents of the drawer. Hesitantly, she reached down and plucked the gold cufflink from atop a folio. Adele studied the image on the rounded edge, her eyes widening.

"It has our family's crest," she observed. "I remember seeing him wear these on several occasions." Adele glanced up. "What shall we do?"

"We must force him to play his hand." Christopher took the cufflink from her palm and replaced it in the desk drawer.

"How?" she asked. Her sweet lips turned in a pensive frown.

"Tonight, Miss Prescott will make her grand entrance," he said with a smile. "I have no doubt that Longmont will incriminate himself after your sudden appearance."

"There must be some explanation," Adele protested. "I cannot believe my uncle would do such a monstrous thing."

"Do you remember anything from the night of the fire?" Christopher asked. "Anything that might implicate or exonerate him?"

Adele closed her eyes. "I remember going to the library to read and passing father's study. I heard raised voices. Uncle Magnus' carriage was outside. But the argument shifted to laughter. I thought nothing of it and continued on to the library." She opened her eyes, tears shining in their depths. "I remember waking in the library to the smell of smoke and shouting. I ran into the hallway. The second floor was ablaze. I tried to climb the stairs, but they collapsed. And then nothing but darkness and silence."

"Anything after that? Do you remember seeing anyone during the fire?" Christopher pressed with care, afraid the memories would cause her undue pain.

"No, but I saw a figure near the doorway shrouded in smoke and shadow calling my name before the stairs collapsed." Adele shook her head. "It must have been Jameson."

Christopher nodded. The new information matched what he had seen in her memories. He wished he could take the pain from her, soothe her anxious mind. But that power seemed beyond his control.

He drew her against him in a warm, comforting embrace. "It cannot be easy to accept his involvement, believe me, I understand your reluctance."

"I deserve the truth," she said, leaning her head against his chest. "We both do."

He smoothed a wayward lock of her hair back and pressed a kiss to her forehead. "Tonight, we will uncover it. I swear."

Chapter Fourteen

Elizabeth pinned the last lock of hair into an elegant coif. Adele admired her friend's work in the small hand-held mirror. The dark braids created a band surrounding a blossom of curls nestled upon her head. Soft wisps of hair framed her face, lending her a gentle feminine grace while accenting her wide, dark-rimmed eyes.

"You look like an angel, miss," Elizabeth said with almost a dreamy sigh. She tucked a small white peony into the braid.

"It is your talent that has transformed me." Adele turned to face Elizabeth. "Am I satisfactory?"

Elizabeth nodded before dabbing a bit of rouge on her cheeks and painting her lips a delicate rose pink. "Now for your gown."

Between the two of them, it took little time to lace Adele into her evening gown. The smooth silk brushed against her skin in a familiar caress. She ran her hands along the blue fabric of the bodice, admiring the detail and the craftsmanship of the gown. The color seemed to shift to green in the dim light when she turned. Never had she worn something so fine, or so revealing. She tugged the bodice up a bit as Elizabeth laced it tight.

When Elizabeth stepped around her, Adele held her arms out. "How does it look?"

The glazed expression on her friend's face spoke more loudly than words ever could.

An insistent beep came from the copper tube in the corner of the room. Elizabeth answered the call.

"The carriage is ready. Please inform Miss Prescott." Jameson's voice echoed through the pipe.

"Right away, sir," Elizabeth responded before closing the cap on the end of the tube.

She snatched up the gloves, fan, and wrap sitting on the edge of the bed. Before she handed them to Adele, Elizabeth paused. "I beg of you to take care. Trust no one this evening with the exception of Lord Dorrington, of course."

Adele smiled at her friend's concern even as a smoldering fear burned deep in the pit of her stomach. "I shall be perfectly fine." She took Elizabeth's hands in her own. "Thank you for everything you have done for me. Truly."

Elizabeth's gaze skimmed over her one last time before she shooed her out the door.

Adele descended two floors and paused on the platform just outside the parlor on the second floor. Lord Dorrington waited near the front door with his back toward her. Resting her hand on the rail, she took the first step toward uncertainty.

Halfway down the stairs, Lord Dorrington turned. Their gazes locked and time shifted to a crawl. The air seemed to thicken with the tension between them.

Her foot slipped on the hem of her gown and she pitched forward down the stairs. In an instant, Lord Dorrington was there, his arms wrapped around her, steadying her as she found her footing once more.

"Thank you."

He clung to her for a moment, his spicy scent soothing and inviting.

"I am afraid I am unused to such frivolous garments," she said with a small laugh when he released her. A wave of disappointment surprised her at the sudden loss of contact. Had she forgotten how wonderful he felt pressed against her? It seemed her body remembered. It hummed with desire, begging for more.

"Shall we?" he asked offering his arm.

Adele gave a tilt of her head and slipped her hand over his arm. They stepped out into the brisk evening air. Andrew waited next to the carriage wearing his finest suit. He held her gaze as they approached the carriage. Andrew offered his hand, but Lord Dorrington stepped between them.

"Thank you, Andrew," Lord Dorrington said over his shoulder.

With a nod, Andrew dropped his gaze and waited until they both were seated in the carriage. Once he latched the door, he disappeared to the driver's post.

Adele settled in her seat as confusion stirred in her heart. *Why would Andrew look at her in such a way?* She knew him for all of her life. His feelings for her had been quite vehement when they last spoke in the stables. He loathed her. And yet, his gaze reflected something much different than his perceived animosity.

"You look exquisite this evening, I must say." Lord Dorrington's voice cut through the fog of her thoughts. "That color suits you."

She felt the heat rise in her cheeks. "Thank you, my lord."

"Have we returned to such formal address?" He leaned close in the shadow of the carriage. "I much prefer to hear my given name on your sweet lips."

Her heart pounded at his words. When his breath brushed against her bare neck just below her ear, she closed her eyes in a desperate attempt to regain some control.

"My lord, I insist, in order to maintain appearances this evening, we should exercise restraint." The words fought against everything she wanted, but the reality of their plans for the evening demanded some rational thought. Which proved difficult when his heat lured her closer and his words wrapped their seductive snare around her senses.

He drew away, leaving her adrift in a sea of need.

She cleared her throat and glanced out the window. It took all the strength she possessed to refrain from reaching for him.

"I see you are wearing the pendant," he said, his voice controlled if not a bit curious.

Her hand fell on the chain holding the pendant. She drew it from between her breasts and held it in her palm. "It is my talisman. My luck charm." Memories of her family played in the back of her mind. The pendant warmed in her closed fist.

Lord Dorrington nodded. "It is special, that I grant you." His gaze dropped to the gentle swell of her bosom tucked behind the bodice of her gown. "Be sure to keep it tucked out of sight."

Curiosity piqued, Adele turned to face him. "Why?"

"I would not want anything to happen to it, since it holds such sentimental value." He straightened his cravat and glanced out the window.

A sudden fear of losing it overwhelmed her. "Perhaps I should remove it for the evening to be safe." She reached for the clasp. "Elizabeth tried to tell me it was not suitable to wear with this gown."

Lord Dorrington's hand pressed against her arm, stilling her. "It looks lovely with the gown. Simply be aware."

She dropped her hands into her lap and toyed with the fan. He withheld something. A nagging suspicion settled in her mind. When she turned to ask him why, the carriage rolled to a stop.

"We have arrived." Lord Dorrington turned, his eyes dark and expression serious. "Do not venture from the ballroom. Always remain with a group of people where I can see you. If you encounter anything suspicious, use your fan to signal me. Open and close it twice."

The nervous flutters that began to stir in her stomach took wing throughout her whole body. She nodded.

He covered her hand with his own. "Save me a waltz."

His request lingered in her mind after they drew apart and he exited the carriage.

Andrew stood outside and offered her his hand to step down from the carriage. He leaned close before releasing her hand. "I shall be waiting outside if you should need me."

Adele glanced at him in surprise. Her lips parted, but

before she could speak, Lord Dorrington came alongside her.

"May I have the honor?" he asked with a charming smile.

"You may, my lord," Adele replied taking his arm.

Together they ascended the stairs leading into her uncle's grand London home. It boasted a large ballroom and at least ten bedrooms. Far more than he needed. Her uncle always lived in a lavish style since he had no title to bolster his reputation. His work for the war office gave him quite a bit of wealth and prestige, but it had been her father's death that gave him the title to solidify his place in society as well as Parliament.

Adele suppressed a shiver as they approached the doors. Had Lord Dorrington not been by her side, offering his support, she would have run away. Part of her wondered if this was how the condemned felt when being led to the noose.

She glanced at her companion. His stoic profile betrayed nothing, but his eyes gleamed with purpose. That alone gave her courage. As long as he stood beside her, she felt as though she could take on a tempest.

A pair of footmen opened the doors. The opulence surrounded her, casting a sudden doubt on her resolve. Lord Dorrington pressed a comforting hand over her own where it rested on his arm.

A footman took their names and escorted them into the grand ballroom where all the guests gathered. His voice boomed over the din of the crowd.

"May I present Christopher Underwood, the Right Honorable, Earl of Dorrington, escorting the Honorable Miss Adele Prescott."

The room fell silent as all eyes turned toward them.

Adele swayed but remained calm, her chin raised and her expression soft. Her gaze swept over the room.

The guests parted, and Adele saw her Uncle Magnus and cousin, Owen, walk through the crowd toward her. While Owen's expression spoke of genuine surprise and welcome, her uncle's seemed a bit more skeptical.

She stood firm when he approached. His gaze skimmed over her, eyes narrowed.

"What is the meaning of this, Dorrington?" he asked his voice low. "Who is this woman?"

"My lord, this is your niece, Miss Adele Prescott," Lord Dorrington replied, his tone steady and unyielding.

Uncle Magnus straightened, aware of the eyes and ears of all the guests behind him. "Follow me." He turned and exited the ballroom.

Adele glanced at her cousin, who studied her with interest, his blue eyes gleaming in the lamplight.

A gentle tug on her arm brought her attention back to Lord Dorrington. "Let me speak," he whispered in her ear as they followed her uncle down the hallway.

They reached a room tucked at the end of the hall, far away from the prying eyes of his guests. Adele recognized the masculine décor and the walls lined with bookshelves, her uncle's private study.

Once all four were inside, Uncle Magnus closed the door behind them.

Adele's grip on Lord Dorrington's arm tightened. Perhaps this had been a grievous error in judgment.

Christopher felt her press against him, her grip on his arm betraying her unease with the situation. He anticipated such a welcome and prepared himself for their doubts as to her legitimacy.

Longmont rounded on them. His face twisted in scorn. He glanced between Adele and Christopher, taking them in measure by measure.

"Owen, pour me a drink," he said without looking at his son, gesturing with a wave of his hand.

Owen responded by acquiescing to his father's demand without hesitation. Christopher noted the thin press of his friend's lips as he poured the liquid. Something ate at him, he could tell. When he offered the glass to Longmont, Owen let his gaze linger on Adele.

Christopher wanted to push her behind him, protect her in some furtive way, and yet she was as much a vital part of this as the rest of them. Each had their role and he could only pray it played out to their benefit. Instead, he stood firm and met Longmont's gaze.

"I demand an explanation, Dorrington," Longmont said before taking a drink of the dark liquor.

"An explanation of what? A miracle?" Christopher feigned ignorance. "I found your niece, whom you presumed to have perished in the fire, and returned her to her rightful place in society."

Longmont's scowl darkened. He turned his dark gaze on Adele. "Look at me, girl."

Adele's head snapped up, defiance flashed in her eyes, but she held her bearing well even though he knew she held on by a thread. Reading her expressions became as easy to him as reading her mind.

"You look the part," Longmont said with a nod. "Even though your hair is darker than Adele's and your face is scarred."

She pressed her lips together to keep from retaliating.

"Where have you been these past six months then, niece?" Longmont took another sip of his drink.

"I have been recovering from my injures. Several servants took me in and cared for me." Her voice held strong as she responded, her words measured and clear. "I colored my hair to keep from being recognized."

"Why not come forward?" her uncle asked.

She inclined her head. "I have. Yet here I stand, and you refuse to accept I am who I say I am."

Christopher watched the conversation with amusement and trepidation. He worried their true intentions might be revealed, but he trusted Adele would be selective in her answers to Longmont's questions. He waited and watched the scene unfold.

"Then tell me something only my niece would know." Longmont set his glass aside and folded his arms across his chest.

Adele paused as if searching her memories for something that might convince him. Then, she smiled. "When I was a girl of ten, I was in the stables. One of the grooms lost control of the horse he had been cleaning. It spun, charging for the open doors. I stood in the way." She recalled the story with confidence. "You appeared and swept me aside before the horse could run me down."

Longmont's expression softened upon hearing her tale.

"I disobeyed father and went to the stables instead of attending my lessons." Adele released Christopher's arm and stepped toward her uncle. "I begged you not to tell him. You swore it would be our secret, so long as I obeyed him from that moment on."

"Adele," Longmont said, his voice filled with awe and regret. "Why in the blazes did you not seek me out sooner?"

"I have only just recovered fully." She glanced at Christopher. "Lord Dorrington hired the servants who saved me, and they begged him to help bring me back to my family." A genuine smile graced her lips before she turned her attention back to her uncle.

"You survived, but how?" Longmont studied her as though he were seeing her for the first time in years.

"I fell asleep in the library and when I woke, the house was on fire." Her voice cracked and still she soldiered forward. "I tried to save them, but...the stairs collapsed." She blinked a few times, obviously in a vain attempt to stop the tears pooling in the corners of her eyes. "When I woke, I was safe, but my family was gone."

Owen stepped forward and offered her his handkerchief. She took it with a grateful smile and dabbed the corners of her eyes.

"At least those damned careless servants did something right," Longmont swore.

"Whatever do you mean?" Adele asked her expression innocent and trusting.

Christopher could have cheered for her convincing performance, but he remained silent. Adele knew what she needed to say, so he played his part of silent protector.

"The fire," Longmont said. "They failed to adequately tend the fireplaces and it was determined to be the ultimate cause of the deadly inferno."

It was not uncommon for inattentive servants to be blamed for a fire claiming a home. In fact, in most cases, he would agree the fire was an accident. However, deep in his soul, he knew something sinister hid behind her family's demise.

Adele wiped away the last of her tears. "May they rest in peace," she murmured.

"Come now," Longmont said with a smile. "We should be celebrating your miraculous return."

Christopher noted the strain behind Longmont's joyful announcement. They had been welcomed into the fold, yet a threat of unease began to unravel in his mind.

"Allow us to begin again," Longmont began offering his arm.

Adele hesitated for an imperceptible moment before taking his arm. "Of course, Uncle."

"You cannot fault me for my mistrust." Longmont glanced at him. "There are far too many people in this world who would sell their souls for an advantageous moment of opportunity."

Christopher inclined his head in agreement. "I could not agree more."

Longmont led Adele from the room, leaving him and Owen to trail after them.

"Should you require anything, we are at your disposal, my dear." Christopher heard Longmont say to Adele as they walked down the hall a few steps ahead.

"Why did you not tell me?" Owen asked in a hushed voice.

"I just discovered the truth myself," he said. Although the lie was not far from the reality as it happened.

"She came to you?" Owen fell into step beside him.

"No," Christopher replied, watching Adele and Longmont. "My servants did."

"I see." His friend clapped him on the back. "Thank you for bringing her home."

He nodded. They reentered the ballroom, which fell silent once again at their appearance.

"Ladies and gentlemen, I have a wonderful announcement!" Longmont's voice boomed over the hushed murmurs and gasps. "My niece, Miss Adele Prescott, is alive and has returned to take her place with her family."

The crowd burst into loud chatter and applause, all attention focused on Adele and Longmont. Christopher stood off to the side, watching the events from the shadows. His gaze followed her as Longmont led her through the crowd and made introductions.

Owen stood beside him. "She has changed, that much is certain."

"Time and tragedy have that effect on people." His heart clenched with jealousy and a protective instinct as they flitted from person to person. Every gentleman vied for her attention. He clenched his teeth.

"You never showed the slightest interest in her before," Owen said, studying him.

"Time changes all things," Christopher reiterated. "Where is your lady love? Did you not tell me she would be present this evening?" Turning the subject away from Adele seemed like the safest course of action.

"Ah yes, the lovely Lady Sophia." Owen's focus shifted to the far side of the room. "She has agreed to become my wife. Her father gave me his blessing this afternoon. We are to announce it this evening."

Christopher smiled and shook his friend's hand. "Congratulations. You two will make quite the handsome couple." He spotted the woman who stole his friend's heart being introduced to the woman who captured his own. "Would you pardon me?"

Owen nodded with a mock salute.

The music and conversation rose around him as he crossed the floor to where Longmont stood with Adele. He ached without her by his side. The music slowed as a waltz began to play. Without hesitation, he interrupted the conversation with a gentle hand on Adele's arm.

"If you will pardon us." He nodded to her admirers. "I believe this dance belongs to me." Christopher ignored the pointed stares they garnered.

He led her to the dance floor and drew her into his arms. The crowd, the noise, the chaos fell away leaving them locked in a melodic embrace. In that moment, nothing existed beyond the waltz and the woman he loved.

Christopher wanted nothing more than to take her home and claim her once and for all.

Chapter Fifteen

Exhilaration coursed through her. Lord Dorrington's grip tightened as they fell into the rhythm of the music. He held her against him. His scent teased her, luring her scandalously close. She wished for nothing more than to lose herself in his embrace.

The music created a safe sphere, encasing them from the crowd and their curious gazes. The events of the evening dimmed with every turn pulling her mind back to the moment, to the man before her. He watched her intently.

"You did well," he said, his voice loud enough for her to hear, but low enough for it to be caught up in the music surrounding them.

"My heart is racing," she replied. "What shall we do now?"

His eyes darkened and he licked his parted lips. "We can leave after this dance if you wish."

A thrill coursed through her body. When they kissed earlier that day desperation flared, wrapping its tendrils around her, pulling her deeper. She wanted nothing more than to leave with him, to spend time with him alone away from the madness of the ball and her uncle's watchful eye.

She glanced beyond him to catch the measured gaze of Uncle Magnus. He stood like a sentinel near the exit watching them. Adele turned away, staring at the sway of her skirts.

"Adele." Lord Dorrington squeezed her hand. "Look at me."

All trepidation fell away when their eyes met. A sense of calm confidence washed over her, enhanced by the soft strains of the violin.

"Say the word," he whispered, "and we shall take our

leave."

The promise in his words echoed in his possessive actions. Adele nodded.

His lips curled in a satisfied smile. The music faded and ceased altogether signaling the end of the waltz. Lord Dorrington took her arm to lead her from the dance floor when Owen appeared before them.

"Dear cousin, would you grace me with your company for the next set?" he asked, offering his hand.

Adele glanced at Lord Dorrington. His expression turned stiff and polite, but she saw the indecision warring deep in his eyes. He gave an almost imperceptible nod, placing the decision squarely on her shoulders.

She hesitated for a moment before releasing Lord Dorrington's arm and taking her cousin's hand. "I would be delighted."

Owen smiled and led her to the dance floor.

Adele recognized the dance, a two-step, livelier than the waltz, yet it maintained the intimacy of having one partner. Owen drew her closer than necessary as the dance began.

"I must confess, dear cousin, to being as enchanted with you as the rest of our guests this evening." He leaned close as the steps brought them together. "It seems you have captured their undivided attention."

She noticed the flitting glances and unabashed stares of the aforementioned guests. Her cheeks heated at the realization. During her dance with Lord Dorrington, she had been shrouded by her contentment with his company. However, with Owen, she found herself longing for her former companion.

"You used to love to dance," he said watching her. "And read if memory serves."

"I still love both," she replied with a flustered smile.

Her cousin, while handsome and charming to a fault, could be the most magnificent dancer and well-read gentleman, yet his company paled in comparison to being in

Lord Dorrington's. She smiled politely, biding her time until the song ended. Her feet moved in mechanical synchronization.

"Am I so terrible a partner?" Owen asked with a laugh.

Adele ducked her head as a blush heated her cheeks. "No, sir, quite the contrary. You are a wonderful dancer."

"And yet, your mind is otherwise engaged," he pressed.

"I beg your pardon, sir," she soothed. "It has been quite an eventful evening. I fear I am unaccustomed to so much excitement."

"An understandable reaction." Owen led her into a turn. "I was concerned I had lost my charm." His blue eyes searched her face.

"Not at all," she replied, desperate to return to Lord Dorrington's side. It was as if Owen's attention combined with the rest of the ball's attendees tipped her beyond capacity. She blinked a few times, weakness infusing her limbs. Her body grew warm and the room began to spin.

"Are you well?" Owen asked, bringing the dance to an end.

"My apologies." She pressed her hand to her head. "I need some air."

Owen nodded and led her to the far wall to a set of doors. Together they exited the ballroom, stepping out onto a spacious veranda. The cool air soothed her overheated face. She turned to see Owen's concerned expression.

"Would you like me to fetch you something to drink?" he asked.

Adele nodded. "If you would be so kind."

"Say no more," he said just before disappearing into the ballroom.

The moon peeked from behind the clouds, casting a barrage of shadows through the tall shrubs lining the edge of the porch. She leaned against the railing, her hand pressed against her chest.

A stolen quiet moment infused her with strength once

more. What had come over her, she could not fathom. The music and conversation burbled through the cracked doors. Adele turned away from them.

"Are you well?" a welcoming voice came from behind her.

She spun to find Lord Dorrington standing a few feet away. How had she not seen or heard him? Her mind must have still been clouded.

"As well as can be expected for a woman who has come back from the dead," she teased.

His expression darkened. "What happened?"

"I got a bit overheated is all." She smiled at his concern and closed the distance between them. "There is no cause for concern."

"I shall worry all I damn well please." He growled. "Come, I have the carriage waiting." He grasped her hand and pulled her to the path leading around the side of the house.

"Should we not bid our host adieu?" she asked, breathless at his determined gate. Adele followed behind him through the shadows and lantern light. Her excitement grew with every step.

Lord Dorrington grunted a distorted response and tugged her farther down the path.

Adele spotted the glowing lanterns lining the streets and the carriages waiting. The dark conveyances scattered like shrouded balloons. Her heart beat sped faster, moving from a two step to a polka.

Before they reached the end of the path, he stopped and turned toward her. Without a word, Lord Dorrington motioned for her to wait. She gave a shaky nod and stood in the shadow of the house. He disappeared around the corner. With every moment that passed, Adele grew concerned at his absence.

The clatter of hooves brought her attention to the street. A familiar carriage drew to a stop several paces from where she stood. Lord Dorrington appeared again and took her hand offering her a comforting smile. He led her to the waiting carriage.

Andrew glanced down from his seat at her approach. He tipped his hat and turned back toward the horses.

Once they settled in the carriage, it lurched into motion. Adele rocked against Lord Dorrington, nearly losing her balance. She steadied herself with her hand but pulled it away when she realized it rested on his muscular thigh.

She glanced up at him, embarrassed by her blunder.

Lord Dorrington pulled her into his lap.

Adele let out a surprised yelp and shifted her body against him. His arms tightened around her. She braced her hands against his chest and stared into his fathomless gaze.

All her life she had been taught to behave as a lady should. Knowing the bounds of propriety and what lay beyond terrified her once upon a time. Yet, Lord Dorrington mesmerized her. His presence soothed her agitation, and she relaxed against him.

"We should not..." The protest died on her tongue when he slid his hand along her side. She drew her lip between her teeth. His breath mingled with her own.

She removed her glove and cupped his cheek in her hand. Lord Dorrington leaned into the touch, his eyes drifting closed.

"You consume my every waking thought, possess my every dream," he whispered. His lips hovered above hers, teasing both of their resolves. "The memory of your kiss haunts me, driving to the point of madness."

Her heart filled near bursting at his words for they echoed the same sentiment that burned inside of her. Adele could find no reply other than the sweet press of her lips against his. He sighed and held her tight against him. She wrapped her arms around his neck. The soft and tender kiss deepened. A coiling heat rose between them bringing her to the point of frustration.

The carriage rolled to a stop and a discrete cough outside the door brought her back to reality. She pulled away from him, her head spinning, her body hot and desperate.

Lord Dorrington eased her off his lap and set her aside so he could climb from the carriage. He thanked Andrew and offered his hand to her.

Adele waited until they were safe inside his home to speak. But once the door closed behind them, Lord Dorrington pulled her against him.

"I shall give you this opportunity to choose, for I cannot maintain my gentlemanly behavior for much longer." He exhaled. "Return to your room...or join me in mine."

The thought of being without him made her shake her head.

A look of rejection passed over his face and he released her. "You should retire then."

Adele brought herself close to him once more and smiled. "You misunderstand."

"You said no." He stiffened. "I will not force myself on you."

"I come willingly." She cradled his face in her hands. "If you will still have me."

"I must make this clear," Lord Dorrington said. "Once I claim you, you will be mine just as I will be yours."

A thrill of satisfaction at his declaration piqued her arousal. She wanted him, and nothing could dissuade her.

"Then claim all of me," she whispered.

Lord Dorrington—Christopher, she reminded herself— took her by the hand and led her up the staircase. When they reached his bedchamber, he pulled her inside. Adele stood next to his bed, her fingers tracing the patterns on the bedpost. When he turned to face her, his eyes burned with intent and something much more carnal.

Her grip tightened on the bedpost as he approached, loosening his cravat with every step. With measured movement, he added another article of clothing. He dropped his jacket and waistcoat near the cravat on the floor.

Her mouth watered at the sight of him removing his clothing.

He removed his shoes with ease then trailed his finger over each button of his shirt, revealing his chest with measured grace.

She licked her lips and found her breath shortened at every small movement he made. Her thighs trembled when he unfastened his trousers. She pressed her eyes closed and mumbled a prayer of forgiveness before opening them once more.

Christopher watched her, a smile on his lips, his hands framing the front of his trousers. "Perhaps I should undress you first."

Adele knew she well and truly sold her soul to the devil before her. "Anything you desire."

He stepped closer, leaning in enough so his lips caressed the shell of her ear. "Anything I desire, you say?" His hands rested on her shoulders. "Tonight, my only desire is to taste all of you."

Adele's heart pounded, her body trembled. He unwrapped her, layer by layer. The fine silks, the linens and undergarments, all fell away. Cast aside on a pile, forgotten.

The kiss of air against her bare skin made her shiver. She covered her exposed torso with her arms. Modesty overwhelmed her desire. All that remained were her stockings and the pendant dangling between her breasts.

Christopher wrapped his arms around her from behind, covering her hands with his own. She glanced at them, the strength harnessed beneath a delicate touch. Adele admired the clockwork hand as it lay cool against her pale skin.

Without a word, Christopher caressed her bare arms until she relaxed, allowing them to fall to her sides. She leaned her weight against him, savoring the intimacy of the moment. Having someone hold her, caress, and desire her awoke a part of her soul that had been dormant since her birth. More than that, she trusted him with more than just her body.

His hands skimmed over her stomach. When they cupped her breasts, she moaned his name into the silence. He kissed the sensitive skin below her ear as his eager touch traveled lower. The feather light brush of his metal fingers over her most intimate parts sent her head spinning. He parted her with the other hand and stroked the folds of her sex.

Adele gasped at the sweet invasion. She drew her lower lip between her teeth to keep from crying out at the pleasurable sensations. His fingertip caressed a sensitive area causing her to buck her hips against his hands. His name spilled from her lips in a desperate plea.

"Christopher...Please..." She fought to contain her roiling need.

He turned her in his embrace, capturing her lips in a fevered kiss.

The tension between them reached a boiling point. Adele clung to him, needing to be closer than just skin to skin. She wanted him inside her. She wished for him to possess her body and soul.

Christopher broke the kiss, their breaths coming in short, wild bursts. "Climb onto the bed, my love."

Adele met his gaze, dark and intense. It fueled her passion making her body warmer. She nodded and climbed onto his oversized bed. The soft fabric of the counterpane slid over her skin as she lay in the center of it. Anticipation seized her when the bed dipped below his weight.

She glanced up to see him in his full naked splendor climbing onto the bed next to her. Her gaze traced every line of delicious skin. He stole her breath with each flex of his muscular body. His manhood stood tall and insistent. A tingle of curiosity made her reach out and take him in her hand.

Christopher froze. His body stiffened, his shaft even more ensnared by her delicate grip. He stared down at her, lips pressed together, eyes burning with lust.

Adele stroked him once.

His mouth fell open releasing a soft, "Fuck."

She grinned at the powerful effect she had on him. Adele explored him with her fingertips.

His hand covered hers, stilling her quest. "We have all evening to discover each other, darling." He lay beside her and drew her against his chest. She melted into his kiss once more.

With a gentle nudge, Christopher settled between her thighs and kissed her deeply. He fitted himself to her, the gentle pressure building to a strange fulfillment. As he pushed himself inside, she gasped. A pleasurable discomfort mixed with desire. The invasive pain dulled as he moved. His sweet kiss soothed her worry.

Once he settled fully inside her, he whispered, "You are mine now, love."

She wrapped her arms around him. "As you are mine."

"Forever," he murmured before kissing her hard. He withdrew and thrust, causing a ripple of euphoria to catch her unaware.

With every movement of his hips, Adele shuddered and met him eagerly. Her body pulsed higher and higher until she trembled with a need she could not voice. She whimpered in frustration and Christopher tilted his hips, rubbing against that sensitive area from earlier.

Adele cried out as the ecstasy consumed her. Waves of pleasure ebbed through her body, radiating from where they were joined. She clung to him, her body tightening around his shaft.

Christopher groaned and pressed his forehead to hers. Warmth filled her as he found his release.

The moment stretched for several heartbeats, until Christopher rolled off of her and fetched a cloth near the nightstand.

Dazed, she watched him clean between her thighs.

"Did I hurt you?" he asked, glancing up at her face.

Adele shook her head.

"Good." He used the cloth to clean himself and then rejoined her. Once he gathered her into his embrace, he sighed in contentment.

Silence settled between them punctuated by the ticking of the clock and the soft crackle of the fire in the hearth. Adele always assumed the company of a good book was heaven but sharing such an experience with Christopher may have redefined it in her mind. She snuggled closer to him and kissed his chest.

"I love you," he whispered.

Adele smiled, her heart fit to burst. "I know," she replied. "The feeling is mutual."

The press of her bare skin from shoulder to toe brought a calming sense of peace over him. Christopher spent so long avoiding any physical contact that it felt almost like a sinful indulgence to lay naked with her draped across him. When she nuzzled closer and kissed his chest, the words spilled from his lips uninhibited. They rang true down to his very core.

"I suppose mutual affection will have to suffice," he replied, holding her tight. "Although you must know I have no intention of releasing you without at least proposing my intentions."

She turned to face him, propping her chin on her hands where they rested on his chest. "Wicked intentions, I have no doubt."

Christopher smiled at the playful gleam in her eyes. He stroked her shoulder with his metal fingertips, and she shivered with delight beneath his touch. "If by wicked intentions you mean marriage, then yes, I have quite wicked designs for you, my dear," he teased.

Her eyes widened her mouth parting in surprise. "Christopher, you cannot possibly wish to marry me."

"Why would I not?" he asked studying her expression.

"If I were still Anne, your maid, would you have made your feelings known?" The question held no malice, just curiosity.

Christopher remembered the moments he almost crossed the line as an employer. He both admired and desired her as his loyal servant, and yet, he could not say for certain if he would have proposed marriage to her. He brushed a lock of hair behind her ear.

"I confess that I desired both your company and your affection before I knew of your identity," he said, feeling like the worst cad for bowing to society's dictations. His fingertips trailed over the delicate skin of her neck.

Christopher toyed with chain holding her pendant.

"Would you have surrendered to me?" he asked in response to her silence. Christopher already knew the answer thanks to the mistaken glimpse into her mind a few nights past.

A rosy hue blossomed on her cheeks.

"I will take that as a yes." He chuckled at her modest reaction, even though she lay bare in his company.

"You seem quite confident in yourself, my lord." Adele shifted into a sitting position beside him. She gathered her hair and drew it over her shoulder.

His gaze followed the luscious curve of her shoulder down to the swell of her breasts and the rose tipped nipples. He longed to take them into his mouth. He desired nothing more than to be buried inside her again and feel her come apart in his arms. Need stirred inside him.

The pendant sat heavy between her breasts. He reached out and took it in his hand.

"Dare I show you just how confident I can be?" he asked as he sat up and removed the pendant from around her neck.

Adele watched him set aside the necklace. "What are you

doing?"

"Have a bit of faith in me," he said, even though the thought of revealing his secret brought him close to physical illness. Before he touched her again, Christopher met her curious gaze. "Form an image in your mind."

She graced him with a skeptical arch of her brow before closing her eyes. A look of furrowed concentration creased her flawless skin before smoothing into calm serenity. She opened her eyes once more and nodded.

Christopher laid his hand atop hers. The warmth of her skin and the jolt of his mind joining hers made his heart race. He closed his eyes and concentrated, moving through the sea of memories and random thoughts swimming in her head. The words he longed to hear floated past him, filling him with hope. A smile tugged at his lips.

He focused on the center of her brain. In the center, he found an image of Alistair sitting in his dim study. Grief strikes Christopher at the sight of his friend. It is enhanced by Adele's sorrow. A peaceful warmth surrounded him as he watched the memory unfold. Adele running toward her father, being swept up in his arms. Love permeated his being.

With a sigh, Christopher drew his hand away from Adele and her memories faded into darkness. The complex emotions churning inside of her caused his own mind to riot. Being inside someone's mind took every ounce of energy he possessed, even more so since he learned of his ability to control the experience. He pushed away the scientific curiosity of such an endeavor and the possibilities of his new-found skill.

Adele watched him with curiosity. "Well?"

"You were thinking of your father," he said once he could trust his voice. "He was sitting in his study when you came to greet him. You must have been quite young. Alistair was not yet graying at his temples."

Her eyes widened. She opened her mouth, and then snapped it closed. He saw the spark of disbelief in her eyes.

"A simple parlor trick."

"You love me," he said, recalling the bold words he encountered in her mind.

Shrouded in his fine linens, Adele blushed and glanced away.

Christopher blocked his ability and took her chin in his hand. "Say the words, Adele. I want to hear them."

"How do you know such things?" she asked turning toward him. A sheen of tears reflected in her eyes.

"You once asked why I wear gloves, even in the comfort of my own home." He held his hands before him, palms up. "My touch is cursed."

Adele shook her head. "Cursed? I do not understand."

Christopher snatched the pendant off the nightstand and held it aloft. The weight of it spun and the metal gleamed in the firelight. How could one innocuous object hold so much power over a person? He loathed what it transformed him into and the path it forced him down. Yet—he glanced at Adele and his heart ached—it led him to this very moment.

"This pendant has caused me so much pain," he said. "And yet, it has brought us together."

Adele touched the pendant with her fingertips before taking it. Christopher dropped the chain. She studied the gift from her father for a moment before the realization settled in her mind.

"The metal was not lost in the fire." She turned the pendant over as if seeing it in a new light.

Christopher shook his head. "Your father was a brilliant man. He must have known you would keep it safe."

She enclosed it in her fist and held it against her heart. "So much anguish over a worthless bauble."

"Priceless, actually," he muttered. "That metal is unlike anything I have ever encountered. It conducts both physical and emotional energies, but more than that, it transformed me."

Adele opened her hand, exposing the pendant once

more. "This tiny thing?" Disbelief laced her words. "Transformed you in what way?"

The inevitable moment arrived, but first he needed to hear the words before he revealed the monster inside. "Tell me," he whispered, leaning closer. "Say the words."

Adele reached up and cupped his cheek. "I love you, Christopher."

Relief and elation filled him. He leaned against her touch.

The pendant glowed in her hand. "Why does it do that?" she asked.

"I believe it may be a reaction to your emotions." He took it and replaced the treasured item around her neck.

"How did it transform you?" Her question settled between them once more.

"Your father and I were testing the electrical conductive nature of the metal when something malfunctioned. The surge of electrical force knocked me unconscious." Christopher raked his hand through his hair. "When I woke, your father and Musgrave were kneeling over me. Musgrave pressed his hand to my temple and a pain unlike anything I have ever experienced, even losing a hand, tore my body apart. My mind felt as though it would explode."

Concern and shock warred in Adele's expression. "How horrible."

"I saw everything in that moment." Christopher paused. "Musgrave's life, his memories, his thoughts, unfolded in my mind like a vast sea. Within moments, I was drowning. The pain consumed me. It was not until he drew away to fetch a doctor that my body found relief."

As the story unfolded, sympathy and realization blossomed. Adele moved closer and rested her hand on his.

"From that moment forward, I shunned physical contact," he continued. "The pain was intolerable otherwise."

Adele laid her hand on his heart. "Does this not cause you pain?"

"No," he replied with a reassuring smile. "When you

wear the pendant, I feel nothing but the warmth of your touch." He pulled her into his arms and kissed her lips. "And desire for you alone." He deepened the kiss.

Wrapped in each other's arms, they found bliss once more and chased it until dawn.

Chapter Sixteen

The rattle of iron against iron woke Adele from a delicious dream. She stirred to find herself alone in Christopher's bed. Memories of the evening before began to filter through her mind, drawing heat to her cheeks and a secretive smile to her lips. Again, the noise sounded from near the fireplace.

Adele grabbed the robe draped on the bed and tied it around her. The cold floor against her feet made her shiver and she pulled the robe tighter. Rounding the bed, she caught sight of Elizabeth kneeling before the fire, stoking it with a poker and adding more coal.

"Good morning," Adele greeted her friend, unsure of how she may react to the situation.

Elizabeth turned with a start and dropped the poker. "Morning, I did not mean to wake you." Her friend avoided her gaze, instead focusing on her task at hand with renewed interest.

"Is everything well?" she asked, curious as to her friend's thoughts.

"Aye, miss," she replied with a sniff.

"Elizabeth." Adele settled on the floor next to her and laid a hand on her arm. "Nothing has changed."

Elizabeth faced her, tears welling in her eyes, and shook her head. "Everything has changed," she whispered and wiped the tears away. Coal dust smeared across her cheeks. "Has the master forced himself on you?"

Adele startled at the question. "Absolutely not."

"You are to be his mistress then?" Elizabeth asked.

"No," Adele snapped with disgust.

"You are still in his employ then? As a maid, I mean."

Elizabeth replaced the poker by the fire.

Adele sat speechless. The night she spent with Christopher meant more than just a night of passion. She loved him. He shared his darkest secret with her. He seemed sincere in his proposal to marry her, but was that what she wanted?

"Are you well, miss?" Elizabeth hung her head. "You must beg my pardon for being so forward, but you are my friend. I wish nothing but happiness for you." She twisted a rag between her fingers. "I have seen far too many women fall prey to passion and the consequences that follow."

Adele offered a half-hearted smile. "I understand your concern."

"Lord Dorrington is a good man, but he is often forgetful," Elizabeth continued.

"Where is he?" Adele asked.

Elizabeth nodded toward the door. "He is in his study, I believe."

"Help me dress, will you?" Adele stood.

With haste, Elizabeth stepped into the adjoining room and returned with a somber wine-colored gown with delicate ivory lace trim. "Lord Dorrington had me store your garments in the spare room."

Adele nodded. It made sense he would request such a thing considering she had no space for such garments in her shared room with Elizabeth. Yet she wondered.

Within moments, Elizabeth helped her dress and affixed her hair into a simple chignon. A splash of rosewater refreshed her face. As she passed the mirror, she paused to study her reflection. No longer was she a child, no longer a maid, no longer a homeless orphan hiding in the world.

Straightening to her full height, Adele took a deep breath. Christopher would know her mind.

Adele descended to the floor below and paused just outside the study's closed door. She steadied her trembling hand before knocking.

"Enter," his voice sounded through the wood.

Adele turned the knob and stepped into the study. She closed the door behind her before searching him out.

Christopher sat behind his desk, a pile of papers before him, with a few tucked in his left hand as he read. When he glanced up, he rose to his feet upon seeing her. "I apologize, love." He lay the papers down and rounded the desk to join her. "Did you sleep well?" he asked, taking her hand in his.

Adele nodded, studying him. His eyes, though bright, bore the signs of sleeplessness, and it was apparent he had not yet shaved or taken a comb to his hair even though he wore clean clothing. She lifted her hand to cradle his cheek in her palm.

"Christopher," she said, building up her nerve. "I must ask you a question."

"Anything, my love," he replied with a genuine smile.

"Am I still free to leave? Take my house in the country and disappear from society?" Adele held his gaze and watched the spark of joy fade from his eyes.

He swallowed and glanced down at her hand tucked in his. "If that is what you wish, then I will remain true to our original agreement."

"Do you love me?" she asked her voice soft and steady.

Christopher's head snapped up. Their eyes locked. Fire and desperation burned in his. "I love you with every breath of life that remains in me."

"Do you wish to marry me?" she asked.

"I have never been more certain about anything in my life." He tilted his head and stepped closer. "I wish for nothing more than to have you by my side always."

She breathed in his scent, his warmth surrounded her. He took her into his arms and held her close. A sense of belonging and peace settled deep in her bones. Every concern Elizabeth planted in her mind melted away. Adele could choose her future, and she could only see one with Christopher in it.

"There is no one I trust as I do you, Adele." He kissed her, teasing her lips with his own. She melted against him. "Marry me, my love." The words whispered across her mouth.

Adele pulled away and removed the pendant setting it on the table beside them. Adele wrapped her arms around his neck and replied by kissing him hard, tasting him on her tongue. In her mind, she pictured them together and thought the words, *I will marry you. I love you, Christopher.*

He kissed her, then pulled back. Christopher smiled. "Clever girl."

Warmth wove its way through her body cocooning her with a sense of certainty that this was the right decision. She smiled up at him. "May I tell the staff?" she asked, anxious to tell someone the wonderful news.

"You may," Christopher acquiesced. "But we should wait to tell your uncle until we have had time to arrange details."

"Should we not ask for his blessing?" Adele could not help but wonder what scandals might arise from not including her closest blood relatives.

"Something tells me Lord Longmont has his own agenda when it comes to your future, my dear. I still do not trust he has your best interest at heart." Christopher held her tight. "I say it may be easier to ask forgiveness than beg permission, do you not agree?"

Adele nodded.

"Besides, I do not wish to be parted from you for longer than necessary," he confessed. "I shall begin the necessary arrangements then." Christopher released her with reluctance and held her at arm's length. "Go, tell your friends."

Joy filled her. "Thank you."

"I shall see you when I return," Christopher said with a gentle kiss to her forehead. He returned to his desk and filed the papers into the top drawer.

Without delay, Adele left him to seek out her friends in

the kitchen. Jameson stood near the sink with Margaret, helping her dry dishes. Elizabeth sat at the table cleaning vegetables for the evening meal. Andrew sat near the stairs on a stool nursing a mug of steaming liquid.

Their attention turned to Adele when she burst into the room. Her joy must have been evident for conversation ceased the moment they spotted her.

"Something amiss, my dear?" Margaret asked. She dried her hands on her apron.

"Christopher, I mean, Lord Dorrington, has asked me for my hand in marriage." Adele could hardly contain her excitement.

"Oh, I knew love would blossom between you two," Margaret squealed. She wrapped Adele in an embrace and kissed her cheeks.

Jameson nodded with a smile. "Congratulations, my dear, you deserve every happiness."

Elizabeth hugged her after Margaret stepped away. "I knew he was a good man. Sometimes he just needs a gentle reminder, eh?"

"I wanted to tell you all first," Adele said with tears in her eyes. "You all took me in and cared for me as though I were your blood. And I appreciate that more than you can possibly imagine."

"Oh, love." Margaret wiped the tears from her own cheeks. "You will always be part of our little family."

"Christopher is out making the arrangements now." She wiped her eyes. "We have decided not to tell anyone of our marriage until after it is over. I knew I could trust our secret to you."

"You have nothing to fear from us," Jameson spoke for all of them. The rest nodded in solemn agreement.

Adele turned to see Andrew staring at her. He set his mug aside and left the room without a word. The action stung her pride. Could he not be happy for her? Even though they rarely got along, his rejection of her happy news left her disappointed.

"Pay him no mind," Margaret said with a wave of her hand. "He's in a right foul mood this morning."

"Perhaps I should speak with him," Adele said.

"As you wish, my dear. Congratulations, again, my love." Margaret returned to her dishes singing a lively tune. Elizabeth joined in.

Jameson shook his head and continued to dry dishes as Margaret handed them to him.

The shroud of mourning lifted like a veil of fog in the summer air. Adele took her leave and followed the stairs to where they led to the garden behind the house.

Andrew might not be her true brother, but she valued his good opinion as she would her own flesh and blood.

Moments after Adele's departure, Christopher found himself staring at the notes again. A renewed sense of purpose infused him. He had longed for its return. While before it had been his scientific research, now a future with Adele beckoned him with open arms.

He sifted through the documents Alistair left for him. A smile tugged at his lips when he stumbled across the sketch later used to design the pendant.

The pendant. He rose from his seat behind the desk and crossed the room. Her scent lingered in the place where they embraced. She had been gone minutes and yet it felt as though she remained with him still and yet been gone for hours. How could one fathom such a paradox of emotions?

Her cherished necklace lay on the table beside the wingback chair. When she took it off and used her mind to answer him, well, in all honesty, it made him love her more. She never questioned his ability, never shunned it. Her curious and open mind soaked up his confession without so much as a doubt. Even if she did doubt, she made no spectacle of it.

He picked up the bauble and clenched it in his fist. The metal warmed beneath his touch, almost feeding off his emotions. With a chuckle, he tucked it into his waistcoat pocket for safekeeping. She would realize she left it behind and wish for its return.

Christopher marveled at his renewed ability to block her memories when they touched. Perhaps all it took was time and practice to control the cursed affliction. Who better to practice with than his own wife.

Wife. The word lingered in his mind. He never imagined himself wed before he inherited the title. Even after, his dedication to the study of science left him absent from ballrooms and galas where he would find a suitable bride. It never crossed his mind the woman who would suit him so well would be the daughter of his scientific partner and trusted friend. Fate had grander plans for him than he could have hoped.

Locked in pensive silence, Christopher pondered the future. He returned to his desk and organized the papers before tucking them away. One phrase scribbled on the bottom of the page caught his attention.

Trust no one, not even family.

The words were underlined twice. How had he not noticed them before? Alistair must have been referring to his fall out with Magnus. It would explain the argument Adele witnessed the night of the fire. The only way he could be sure was to call on Longmont and confront him.

Before he could do so, he needed to ensure his attachment to Adele was legal and binding as well as front-page news. Lord Longmont would have no claim on her if she were already bound to Christopher.

He tucked the folio into the top drawer.

With a bit of convincing, he could procure a marriage license in a short period if he began the process that afternoon. With his mind set to the task, Christopher took a comb from the side drawer and fixed his hair. A glance in the side mirror confirmed he required a shave as well.

He crossed to the copper tube and pressed the keypad for the kitchen.

"You rang, my lord." Jameson's voice echoed through the tube.

"Yes, I require a shave. Please ensure I have hot water drawn."

"Very well, my lord." The line disconnected.

Once he was assured of his hair being presentable, Christopher returned to his desk to replace the comb. He brushed his hand over his stubble once more. It would be quite a relief to not have to shave himself anymore. First, he needed to learn to control his ability to an adequate level. He had no wish to read his butler's mind.

He reached for the closed door when it opened beneath his hand. Jameson stood before him with Owen standing just behind his right shoulder.

"My apologies, my lord, Mr. Prescott to see you." Jameson stepped aside, his expression betraying nothing but professional courtesy. "Do you still require a shave, my lord?"

"Yes, Jameson, I shall be with you directly." He nodded at the butler, who then took his leave.

"Going somewhere, old chap?" Owen asked with a carefree grin as he stepped into the room.

"I have business to attend," Christopher replied with a measured tone. Irritation filled him at being delayed on such an important errand. "What brings you around?"

"Can I not call on my old friend?" Owen spun the walking stick in his hand. "Especially after such a shocking revelation last evening, followed by a hasty retreat."

Christopher remembered the ball, and yet it all seemed a distant and irrelevant memory after the evening he spent with Adele. He almost forgot their revelation was part of a much grander plan.

Christopher nodded. "Of course."

"Come now, my friend, modesty does not suit either of us." Owen crossed to the decanter of whisky and poured himself a drink as well as one for Christopher. "How did you find her?" Owen offered the glass.

He studied the liquid in the glass but did not drink. "She came to me asking for my aid."

"When was this?" Owen asked before sipping the amber liquid.

"Several days ago," he admitted. Not that Owen deserved to know any other details, but Christopher felt the prying questions of Lord Longmont filtering through his son. He treaded carefully with his answers.

"Where has she been staying?" Owen asked. "I mean, where is she now? My father has sent me to find her and bring her home."

"So, this is not a visit from a friend, is it?" Christopher set the glass aside.

"Come now, you cannot blame me." Owen raised his hands in supplication. "I am only the messenger sent to do my father's bidding."

"Miss Prescott is safe and well cared for at the moment." He noted Owen's carefree expression, even though his narrowed gaze belied tension. "And your father can hardly call his home her own since hers is lying in ash and ruin."

Owen drained the contents of his glass. "Your point is made, my friend. You do not believe my father has the best intentions laid for my cousin. And you may well be right in that assumption."

Christopher crossed his arms. "What do you mean?"

With a sigh, Owen poured another drink. "Father has had three offers for my cousin's hand this morning alone." He shook his head. "All from prominent men who represent a great interest to my father."

"So, Lord Longmont is willing to sacrifice the happiness of his niece for his own personal gain?" Rage roiled through his blood. The thought of Adele being auctioned off to the highest bidder infused him with fury and indignation, not to mention jealousy. He would rather hang than see her married off to solidify Longmont's selfish union to some wealthy old man.

"I am not pleased with this turn of events either," Owen confessed with a frown. "Father has always been a man with lofty pursuits. His determined nature has earned him much in life, and yet it costs him more than he realizes."

Christopher strode to the window and glanced down into the garden. This madness could be silenced with his elopement to her. If he could buy some time to secure their attachment, then Longmont would have no control over her.

"Where is she, Dorrington?" Owen asked, his voice echoing in the room.

A familiar woman clad in a wine-colored gown emerged from the stables and crossed the yard toward the house. She disappeared from view and fear tugged at Christopher's heart. Owen would see her.

"I cannot say for certain," he lied. "If you will pardon me, I must see to my business before the morning is lost."

Owen set aside the glass and nodded. "I detest this as much as you. Truly, I only wish the best for my cousin."

"Thank you for your concern," Christopher said as he led Owen from the room and down the stairs.

Upon arriving at the front door, Owen turned. "You know where to find me should you change your mind. Father will not be pleased."

"Then he can call on me himself." Christopher's renewed vigor seemed to take Owen by surprise.

He smiled before donning his hat. "Good day, my friend."

With a nod, Christopher closed the door behind him. Once he steadied the racing of his heart, he ascended the stairs to his room where Jameson waited for him.

Time was of the utmost importance, and he wasted

enough of it already.

164 Kirsten S. Blacketer

Chapter Seventeen

Adele stepped into the muted sunlight and inhaled the sweet scent of the new flowers blooming in the spring garden. She lifted her skirt to walk along the pathway leading to the stables.

As she approached, she heard a clatter arise inside the stable. The heavy scent of horses and leather greeted her when she stood in the doorway. Her eyes adjusted to the dim lighting.

In the far corner, Andrew's broad figure stood next to an open stall.

Adele entered with caution, not wanting to startle the horses.

"Andrew," she called softly.

He stilled, his body stiffened at the sound of his name. Without a word he resumed his work spreading fresh bedding in the stall.

She crossed the distance between them. A pang of guilt and pain tugged at her heart. Why did he always have to treat her with such disdain? "Andrew," she said again.

The handsome stable hand turned and leaned against his pitchfork. "What do you want?"

"I want to know why you are cross with me," she asked. "Why do you treat me as though I am nothing more than a stain on your boot?" Adele sighed. "What have I done to earn your censure?"

He scoffed and returned to his work with renewed vigor. "I doubt the good opinion of the hired help is worth your concern. Return to the house, *miss*." The title slid from his tongue in a mocking tone.

"Not until you answer me," she demanded.

When he ignored her, she reached for his arm. He spun around, dropping the pitchfork and pinning her against the stall door.

"You delight in putting yourself in harm's way at every turn, but there will not always be someone to protect you." His broad body blocked her from seeing anything but him.

She met his dark eyes, her mouth parted in surprise. "I do not put myself in danger."

His lips twisted in a cynical smile. "This whole charade, playing maid and reemerging into society, not to mention your engagement to Lord Dorrington. You are playing a very dangerous game."

Fear skittered down her spine. She knew Andrew would never bring her harm. Would he?

"What do you mean?" she asked her voice low and trembling.

He scoffed. "You cannot see anything beyond your own precious world, can you?" He shook his head. "Last evening, a carriage followed you and Lord Dorrington from the ball to this house."

"Someone followed us?" Adele froze at the implications of his words.

"They were parked at the end of the street when I pulled the carriage around," he continued. "It was unmarked."

"You must tell Lord Dorrington," she said realizing the dire consequences this could bring.

"You tell him," he said before releasing her. "I will not concern myself for your safety any longer."

"Andrew." She reached for his arm. He froze beneath her touch. "What do you mean by that?"

He paused for a moment before speaking. "Sometimes this feeling of dread comes over me, and I cannot ignore it. Last evening, that feeling manifested again. This day, it is stronger than ever." He faced her again. "You are in danger, of this I am sure."

Adele could not laugh, not when she recognized the

serious tone of his voice and the steely glint in his eyes. "How can you be sure?"

He raked his hand through his hair. "The night of the fire, I had the same feeling." He paused. "I ran to the house to find it engulfed in flames. When I ran inside, I found you lying at the base of the stairs unconscious."

"You saved me?" she whispered. The realization stunned her. She never knew who pulled her from the house that night. Andrew saved her from certain death.

"I could not save my sister or your family," he said with a shrug. "But I could not let you die. That night, I learned to listen to my instincts, and they have not led me astray."

Andrew's words brought emotion bubbling to the surface. Adele pressed her hand to her chest, speechless at his confession.

"I harbor no ill will toward you." His voice softened. "Curse me for a fool for caring too much." He squared his shoulders and maintained distance between them. "I saved you once. Do not expect me to do it again." He added in a hushed whisper, "You are not mine to protect."

Adele drew in a sharp breath at his words. "Oh, Andrew." Tears threatened to fall at his words and the lost expression on his face.

She reached for him but he drew away and shook his head.

"You should return to the house," he said stiffly. "Do not concern yourself with me, miss." With a forced smile, he returned to his duties.

"Thank you again for saving me." Adele let her hands fall to her side and held her chin up. "I shall forever be in your debt, *brother*."

Before she could embarrass herself further, Adele strode from the barn. The sunlight warmed her face. Determined, she crossed the garden and entered the house. Once inside, she leaned against the door and closed her eyes. How could she compose herself after such a confession?

Shaking her head, Adele stole up the servant's staircase toward her shared room with Elizabeth. Once she made it to the confines of her chamber, she latched the door and sat at the foot of the bed.

Andrew saved her. Not just that, but he harbored feelings for her. Feelings he would rather bottle up inside than reveal to the world. He loved her as more than a sister or a friend. She pressed her hands to her lips.

Not only had he lost his family in the fire, but he lost her by consequence as well. Even though she viewed him as a friend and in a brotherly fashion, guilt consumed her for not reciprocating his love. She pushed it away. Andrew made no overt declarations or promises. His simple confession meant to convey one thing alone, and that was the surety of her safety which would be Christopher's concern since their engagement.

"Oh, dear Andrew, I am truly sorry." A tear slipped down her cheek. "I must speak to Christopher when he returns." She wiped the tears away. "He must know the truth, and we must find out who is behind this."

In the stillness of her chamber, Adele pondered what Andrew said about the carriage the evening before. They rattled something loose with their grand revelation. Could it possibly be her uncle? Would he stoop so far as to have her followed?

Adele reached for the pendant tucked within her gown. Her fingers touched the bare skin where it would have been. She gasped. Had she lost it somehow? Then she remembered. Christopher and his study. She removed it so he could read her mind.

An insane thought really, the ability to read one's mind. She never would have been open to the possibility of such a thing had it not been for her fondness for novels and her father's love for science. He always told her to believe the impossible, no matter how improbable. With physical proof, it was difficult to deny the truth.

Christopher truly had the ability to read minds. Her mind.

Knowing he was no longer home, Adele retreated to his study to wait for his return. She must clear her conscience. With a man who can see into one's mind, honesty seemed the best course of action to prove her love.

Procuring a marriage license on short notice proved to be a taxing endeavor, and yet Christopher was able to do so with the aid of his title and a small donation of funds. Within the week, he would be wed to Adele, and no one save God Himself would be able to stop their union.

He climbed the stairs to the front door of his townhouse and met Jameson in the hallway.

"Ah, yes, Jameson, please send Otis up with a fresh pot." He handed his hat and walking stick to Jameson who nodded.

"Yes, my lord." He backed away with a bow. "Miss Prescott is waiting for you in your study."

Christopher smiled. The very person he longed to speak with. He remembered seeing her leaving the stables and the uncomfortable conversation with Owen about Longmont's plans for her. A long conversation over a pot of tea was exactly what he needed at that moment.

He climbed the stairs and opened the door to his study. Adele sat in his oversized chair by the fireplace with her face hidden behind a book. He closed the door with a soft click.

For a moment he studied her. Lost in an imaginary world, she seemed engrossed by the words on the page, enough so that she did not notice his arrival.

Otis dinged and his doors slid open, heralding the procurement of tea.

Adele peeked over her book at the dumbwaiter and smiled when she spotted Christopher leaning against the wall watching her. "How long have you been standing there?" she asked setting her book aside.

"Long enough," he replied. Pushing away from the wall, Christopher retrieved the tray from Otis and set it on the small table between her chair and the empty one opposite.

"Allow me." She poured the tea and handed him the cup and saucer.

Christopher sat down, his gaze resting on her fluid, confident motions. The idea of her being like this every day warmed him with a comfortable sense of happiness. He rested his hand on the papers tucked in his jacket pocket before reaching for the cup she offered.

He would marry her before the week's end. The warmth of the tea stung his lips. He could only hope Longmont would not discover her location before the nuptials could be performed. Perhaps the next morning would suffice for their union.

Adele seemed distant. Her gaze lingered on the fire flickering in the hearth. The tea sat cradled in her hands, untouched.

"Something amiss, my dear?" Christopher asked, pushing his own thoughts aside.

She snapped from her reverie with a smile. "Of course not."

"Have you informed your friends of our good news?" He set the cup in the saucer and replaced it on the tray.

"I have." She sipped her tea. "They are overjoyed at our impending marriage."

"As they should be," Christopher said with confidence.

The smile fell away from her lips. Her gaze lost in the fire once more.

"I take it someone has not accepted your glad tidings well?" He leaned back in the chair and studied her.

Adele sighed and set the cup down with a soft clatter. Agitation highlighted her actions.

"I saw you leaving the stables earlier," Christopher observed. "Your *brother*," he emphasized the word with dulcet tone, "did not take the news well, I gather."

"Andrew," Adele murmured, meeting Christopher's gaze. "He seemed upset by our engagement, so I ventured to the stables to speak with him."

Christopher leaned forward when he caught sight of the blush creeping along her neck up into her cheeks. "Has he accosted you?" He leapt to his feet. "I shall toss him into the streets myself if he so much as harmed a hair on your head."

Adele rose and rested her hand on his arm. "No, no, he has done nothing of the sort. Please." The pressure of her hand increased with her grip. "You must understand."

He relaxed under her touch. Uncertainty and frustration clawed at him. He should have kept her close, but in reality, he knew it would be an impossibility until they were wed.

"Andrew and I have known each other for years. We used to play as children," she explained, her voice soothing and calm. "His sister became my ladies' maid." She paused. "He taught me to ride a horse with confidence after I had been thrown from the saddle."

Christopher pulled his arm from beneath her hand. "You have feelings for him then."

"Of course, I do," Adele said with exasperation. "How could I not? He is like part of my family."

"Does he love you?" Christopher asked. He braced himself, wondering how he could have been so blind.

"Enough to know that I am happy with you, that I love you, and I am exactly where I need to be," Adele explained. "I do not love him as he does me." She stepped closer. "I love you alone, Christopher."

He saw the earnest fire in her eyes and held out a hand for her. She closed the distance between them and wrapped her arms around him. Christopher savored the sweet scent of her and held her tight.

"He saved me," she whispered. "The night of the fire. Andrew pulled me from the inferno. He carried me to safety."

Her words rang with truth. Words he heard Andrew use

himself to describe how he had saved his sister. Christopher felt the concern give way to gratitude. He held her for a moment before leaning away enough to tip her chin up, forcing her to peer into his soul.

"For his loyalty and his act of bravery, I will allow him to live unscathed." He brandished his words like a weapon. "But so help me, if he touches you again, I will make sure even God himself will not find the remains."

Adele's eyes widened, her mouth gaped in shock.

"Mark my words, my love." He leaned closer. Their breaths mingled. His mouth watered for a taste of her. "You belong to me, body and soul, and no man shall ever steal you from me. Do you understand?"

Heat blossomed between them.

Adele nodded. "I expect the same loyalty, my lord."

Christopher grinned. "You shall have no fear on that count, darling. No one can come between us. Not even your uncle."

"My uncle?" She drew back, curiosity furrowing her brow.

"Yes, Owen visited this morning in search of your location." Christopher brushed an errant curl behind her ear. "It seems your uncle has decided to take you into his loving home under his benevolent care." He paused for a moment before continuing. "Needless to say, I lied about your whereabouts."

"I thought you were close friends with my cousin?" she asked. "He would know you better than most, especially if you were lying to him."

Christopher pondered her observation. While valid, he shook his head with certainty. "Owen claimed to be the messenger. I imagine he has already informed his father of the situation and returned to his own amusements."

Adele seemed to be lost in thought, but she remained cradled in his embrace.

"Do you wish to be returned to your uncle?" he asked

fearing her answer.

She tightened her hold on him and leaned her head against his chest. "No, I am right where I wish to be."

Relief consumed him. He reached into his pocket and withdrew the papers he garnered that morning. "I must admit, this would have been a worthless investment had you said yes." He handed her the folded documents.

She pulled away and opened them. Joy filled her expression as she read. She glanced up with tears gleaming in her eyes. "We are to be married." Adele glowed.

It took all of his strength not to pull her into his arms and kiss her senseless. "We are. In the morning, if that is your wish."

Adele laid the papers down on the chair and threw herself into Christopher's arms. He caught her with delighted surprise.

"Thank you," she whispered before kissing him on the mouth.

Christopher moaned when she clung to him, her warm mouth coaxing his into submission. He pulled away when her mind began to bond with his. He could not contain his abilities when she enchanted him so completely.

He reached into his pocket and removed the pendant. "Unbutton your blouse," he said, his words laced with desire.

Adele drew her lower lip between her teeth as she obeyed him. Her gaze locked with his. His heart pounded with every button that slipped from its mooring revealing her creamy skin.

He licked his lips as she pulled the blouse open. The tops of her breasts rose with every breath.

When he looped the chain around her neck, the pendant lay tucked between the glorious orbs he longed to taste. With measured restraint, Christopher peeled the blouse from her, dropping it onto the floor. He cupped the back of her neck as he lowered his mouth to the top of her left breast.

No memories assaulted him, no thoughts from her mind,

only the pure bliss from loving her.

Adele sighed at his touch. She leaned against him.

He peppered kisses along her skin, delving his free hand into her corset and releasing her breast. She gasped and her hands tightened in his hair when he pulled her nipple into his mouth.

Heavens above, but he wanted her with a ferocity that defied comprehension. He freed her other breast and laved attention between them. Careful of each step, he backed her against his desk.

He gathered her skirts in his hands and lifted them around her waist.

"Lie back on the table, love, let me taste you." He slid his fingers along the delicate seam of her sex.

Her surprise was matched by the ferocious hunger driving the moment of passion.

Chapter Eighteen

A wave of embarrassment followed by pure need swept over Adele. She bit back a gasp when he touched her center. With the skirts bunched around her waist, she sat on the desk and laid back.

Apprehension and excitement filled her. She could not see him beneath the mass of fabrics, but she felt every touch, every breath he took. His hands slid along her inner thighs, spreading her wide. His breath brushed against her wet sex.

Adele bit her lip to keep from crying out.

When his mouth descended on her, she bucked against him. "Christopher!"

Restraint snapped as he lapped at her folds. Pleasure buzzed through her with every stroke of his tongue, every soft caress of his fingers. She tossed her head from side to side. He devoured her, bringing unbelievable bursts of delight hurtling through her body. When she thought she could no longer stand the pressure, Christopher slid his fingers into her, curling them against her walls.

"Oh, sweet merciful heavens." Adele gasped the words on a breathless moan then shattered from the onslaught of attention. Her body pulsed around his fingers, against his tongue. Bathed in orgasmic bliss, Adele wilted against the desk.

Christopher chuckled when he peered over her skirts. "I am far from finished with you, my sweet."

He drew her up and kissed her. She found her passion stirring again and clung to him, desperate for more. He unfastened his trousers and freed himself. Pressing his cock against her entrance, he claimed her once more.

His kiss became frenzied, matching the thrusts of his

hips. Adele wrapped her legs around him. He drove deeper into her bringing her close to the edge of the desk.

Leaving a trail of kisses along her jaw and down her neck, he explored her body. When his lips closed around her nipple, she tightened around him. A groan broke the silence in the study. She could not tell if it was his or hers, but it mattered not. Both of them became lost in the moment of sensual bliss.

He leaned back as he thrust into her. The pendant bounced against her breasts with every thrust. It warmed against her skin, glowing. As their passion increased, so did the brightness and warmth of the pendant.

Christopher drew her close. His heat seeped into her, feeding her need, her desire. She returned the fervor, her body tensing with the building pleasure. He angled his hips and ground them against hers. An explosion of delight ripped through her body.

Adele clung to him, breathless and panting. When he reached his climax, he buried his face against her breasts and murmured her name over and over.

She smiled and stroked his hair.

He glanced up at her, his cheeks warm and pink from exertion. He glowed with satisfaction. She imagined she looked much the same. Warmth flooded her face.

"Did I hurt you?" he asked with obvious concern.

Adele drew him close and kissed his soft lips. "Not at all."

He withdrew a handkerchief from his pocket and cleaned himself as well as her. The thoughtfulness brought a tug of sentiment. How she loved him.

"My apologies," he said, helping her to her feet. "It was not my intention to seduce you in my study."

"I quite enjoyed the seduction," she replied with a smile. Adele tucked herself back into her blouse. "I do have one request however."

"Name it and it shall be yours." He smoothed his hair

back.

"Next time I wish to taste you." Her words surprised herself, but the look on Christopher's face made her laugh. He seemed equal parts shocked and aroused.

He cleared his throat. "Well, I have no objections to that. But we should continue our explorations in my bedchamber, after a hot bath and some sustenance, I believe."

Adele crossed to the small brass box and copper pipe. She pressed the button to the kitchen.

"How may I be of service?" Jameson asked through the other end.

"Would you draw a bath in Lord Dorrington's chamber, and please have Otis deliver supper there as well when it is ready?" She watched Christopher while she gave the instructions.

"As you wish, miss," Jameson responded before disconnecting the line.

"You are fortunate he likes you," he said with a lopsided grin.

"Fortune has nothing to do with it." Adele laughed.

Christopher caught her up in his arms. He brushed a tender kiss on her forehead. "Come, let us forget the world for a while."

He caught her by the hand and led her from the study, up the stairs and into his bedchamber where he proceeded to teach everything a proper lover should know.

Hours later, Adele lay in bed, the darkness pierced by the light from the fire. Sated by a long evening of carnal pleasure, she should have been exhausted. And yet sleep eluded her.

She glanced over at Christopher, who lay in a deep slumber. Perhaps she exhausted him instead of the other way around. Adele pressed a soft kiss to his cheek and slipped from the bed.

Careful not to disturb him, Adele donned her nightgown and robe, followed by a pair of slippers. She lit a lantern and without making a sound, crept from the room and down the staircase.

A book would soothe her mind enough to find sleep. She made her way to the study. The memory of what transpired there earlier brought a heat to her face. After such an encounter, embarrassment should have been a thing of the past, and still she blushed.

Once inside, Adele set the lantern on the desk. A fire burned low in the hearth, barely lighting the room. She searched the shelves for a novel that might catch her fancy.

"Perhaps Ms. Austen will soothe my mind this evening." She pulled a leather-bound tome from the shelf.

A series of beeps startled Adele. She spun to find Otis' doors sliding open against the far wall. He chirped once before waiting with open compartment.

She laughed and pressed her hand to her chest to still the thundering of her heart. "You silly contraption," she said with love.

He beeped once more before silence descended.

Then she heard it. The creak of the stairs echoed through the crack in the door.

Adele extinguished the lantern light and crouched down behind the desk.

Her heart pounded. The door groaned as it opened.

Perhaps it was Jameson. Or Christopher. She pinched her eyes closed and waited for the interloper to speak.

The soft shuffle of boots on the thick carpet alerted her to their presence, and yet they did not speak. Maybe an intruder came to steal Christopher's research. She opened the drawer and removed the folio from where she seen him place it.

In the dark, she crept to where Otis' doors sat open and placed the folio inside. Once she pressed the button it would alert the intruder to her presence, but she had to keep Christopher's research safe.

She licked her lips. The door lay wide open. She spied the tall, broad figure of the thief against the far window as they crept closer to the desk. Certain she could make it out the door and alert the household she pressed the button, sending Otis up to Christopher's chamber.

With a series of beeps and a mechanical whirr, Otis ascended.

The intruder spun around and spied her.

Adele rose to her feet and bolted toward the exit.

She yelped as a pair of strong hands latched onto her arm, jerking her back into the room. She stumbled and fell against the intruder. When she moved to scream, a hand covered her mouth. Wildly twisting against him, she struggled to free herself. She shoved her elbow into his side.

He groaned and she broke free. Her foot caught the hem of her nightgown and she fell headfirst against the tall copper inverter dominating in the corner of the study. Pain spiked through her head and shoulder before the darkness consumed her.

Christopher curled deeper into the mattress. Somewhere in the back of his mind his consciousness stirred. He cracked his eyes open breaking from sleep.

An insistent beeping echoed through his chamber rousing him. He reached for Adele but found a cool void where she should have been in bed beside him. He furrowed his brows with concern. Perhaps she went to fetch a drink or a book from his study.

The beeping continued from the far wall. Christopher pushed himself up and out of bed. Crossing the room, he found Otis' doors open, the obnoxious beeping coming from the frustrating machine.

"Alright, Otis, very well, you have my attention." He spoke the words even though he knew the machine could not possibly understand him. Yet the noise ceased.

Christopher noticed the contents of Otis' carriage. His folio of scientific notes, more specifically, the notes on his mysterious metal. Upon removing the folio, Christopher realized the reason for Otis' sudden appearance.

Adele.

Without delay, he donned his robe and trousers before darting down the dark staircase to his study below. The darkened room proved hazardous in the dark. Yet he located the lamp sitting on his desk and lit it.

Christopher's heart stopped. His office had been ransacked. Papers lay scattered on the floor, chairs overturned, and his inkwell smashed against the wall. The dark smudge smeared like a bloodstain down to the carpet.

He searched the room but found no sign of Adele. He called for her knowing it would be futile. She was nowhere to be found.

Agitated and terrified, he raked his hand through his hair.

Jameson. Without a moment's hesitation, he ran to the intercom and rang his most trusted servant.

"Yes, my lord," came Jameson's tired voice.

"Come to my study quickly!" he barked, trying to keep the fear from his voice. "Adele is missing."

Within two minutes, Jameson, Margaret, and Elizabeth stood in the doorway of his study.

"What happened, my lord?" Jameson asked, stepping into the room.

Christopher looked up from the mess scattered across his desk. "As far as I can gather, someone came for my notes and found Adele instead." He smoothed his hand across the stubble on his jaw.

"Margaret and Elizabeth, check the rest of the house. We need to be assured Adele is not here before we summon the police." Jameson's calm instructions soothed Christopher. "Rouse Andrew as well. Have him report to me."

The two women nodded in unison and disappeared from view.

"My lord," Jameson said his voice calm and soothing. "Is

anything missing aside from Miss Prescott?"

Christopher shook his head. "No, the thief took nothing." His head ached from the implications of this botched robbery. "Do you think they took her?"

Fear coiled in the pit of Christopher's stomach. He should have hired more staff. Someone to keep watch while they slept. He feared their revelation would rouse the initial thief to action, and he had been right. Unfortunately, Adele was caught in the middle of the disastrous plan.

"Damn it!" Christopher shouted, pounding his metal fist on the desk. The wood splintered beneath the force of the blow.

Jameson cleared his throat. "I may have found something, my lord."

Christopher dropped to his knees where Jameson knelt on the carpet beside his energy inverter. It hummed behind him.

"I believe this belongs to Miss Prescott," Jameson said lifting a familiar chain holding Adele's pendant.

He snatched it, holding it up to the light. The chain had been torn, yet the pendant seemed to be intact. It warmed in his palm as his held it tight.

"There is some blood here, my lord." Jameson pointed to the cylinder behind him.

A smear of red stained the copper finish. Enough to show someone had been wounded in what he could assume was a struggle.

"Send for a detective from Scotland Yard, Jameson." Christopher rose to his feet and tucked the pendant into his pocket.

"At once, my lord," Jameson said. The butler rose to his feet and exited the room.

Christopher collapsed against the wall cursing himself a fool for thinking he could protect her. The whole charade had been his plan. If only he had been more vigilant.

"My lord," Andrew's voice broke through the

momentary onslaught of guilt.

"Miss Prescott has disappeared." Christopher straightened and faced Andrew. "You would not happen to know where she could be."

Surprise etched the young man's features. "No, my lord. How would I know—"

Christopher charged him, knocking the youth back into the wall and pinning him there. "I know you love her. If you hurt her in any way, I swear this day will be your last." Rage simmered inside him. His grip on the young man tightened.

Andrew shook his head but met Christopher's stare full on. "'Tis true. I love her. Enough to let her choose her own fate." He pushed at Christopher's hands, budging them a little. The young man scowled at him. "I do not know where she is, damn you!"

"Why should I believe a word that spills from your mouth?" Christopher snarled.

"Because I care for her as much as you and I would *never* wish her harm." He relaxed a fraction, realizing his situation. "Let me help you find her. I beg of you."

Truth rang in Andrew's words, and with reluctance, Christopher released him.

He swore under his breath before turning away.

Andrew took in the state of the study. "Did she inform you of the carriage?"

"What carriage?" Christopher asked his curiosity piqued.

"After the ball, an unmarked, black carriage followed us from Lord Longmont's estate. It parked at the end of the street." He shook his head. "I informed Adele of the suspicious carriage yesterday morning with instructions to convey my concerns to you."

Christopher frowned, his mind spinning at the possibilities.

"My apologies, my lord, I should have brought my concerns directly to you." Andrew bowed his head.

"There is nothing to be done for it now, Andrew." He crossed to his desk and righted his chair.

Christopher sighed, glimpsing the azure glow of predawn filtering through the windows. Somewhere out in the chaos of London, Adele lay in hiding. He damned well would find her even if he had to tear the city apart one stone at a time.

"What would you have me do, my lord?" Andrew asked breaking the silence.

"Ready the carriage," he said. "I shall engage some aid in our search."

With a nod, Andrew left him alone.

She could not have been taken far. There were already vendors filling the streets and merchants rousing for their day. One would have observed a woman being taken against her will.

Unless it was someone close. Someone who wanted her returned to her family with due haste. *Longmont.* The man's name sent a shiver of fury coursing through his veins. He never imagined Lord Longmont would stoop so low as to kidnap his own niece.

Christopher prayed he was right. It proved to be the only logical conclusion. Longmont wanted her under his roof, under his control, so he took her by force.

Jameson appeared, this time dressed impeccably and standing at attention. "I have summoned the appropriate authorities, my lord. Margaret and Elizabeth have searched the house. There is no sign of Miss Prescott." A glint of fear deep in his eyes belied the butler's polished persona.

"Help me dress, Jameson," Christopher said with resolve. "I shall be paying an early call on Lord Longmont."

Chapter Nineteen

Agonizing pain knifed through her head. Adele opened her eyes to find dark fabric blinding her vision. A strip of fabric lay across her tongue. She choked when she attempted to call for help. The dry air made her cough. She tried to swallow what little spit remained, but it proved fruitless. Propped in a chair, Adele's body protested with every movement as she attempted to free herself.

Her arms refused to budge as well as her legs. Panic clawed at her chest. She pulled again, the restraints tugging against the delicate flesh of her wrists and ankles. The bastard had not only blindfolded and gagged her but bound her as well. *How original,* she thought remembering a similar scenario from a book she once read.

The humorous thought gave way to panic once more as the reality of her situation broke over her like a bucket of freezing water. A small sob wrenched itself from her throat.

A familiar barrage of sounds made her still. The echo of shoes on hardwood, the creak of a squeaky door hinge, and the distinctive click of a lock closing. She noticed other things. The tick of a clock, the unmistakable aroma of leather and books, the lingering notes of tobacco and whiskey betraying a man's apartment. A very wealthy man.

She recognized the scent. Her uncle's study. Surely, he would not have been so foolish as to kidnap her.

Adele waited, knowing she was not alone, refusing to show even the slightest hint of weakness. The bastard wanted to instill fear, and so he had, but she would never let him see how it affected her.

Tobacco smoke tickled her nose. Her uncle always favored his pipe.

She opened her mouth to speak, but her words emerged a garbled mess through the gag.

Warm fingers trailed along her scarred jaw. She flinched at the contact, attempting to pull away. The gag slipped from her mouth when his fingers hooked the fabric and tugged it free.

Adele struggled for a moment to moisten her mouth. The words built like a raging river behind a dam. Once she composed herself, she released her vehemence. "Release me at once!" She struggled against her bonds. "You have no right to do this to me, Uncle. Release me!"

Her breathing became agitated and frustration consumed her. She never anticipated the laughter that met her ears. The slow, deep rumble of amusement made the hairs on her arms stand on end. "Do I amuse you, Uncle?" she asked her voice steady even though her body trembled.

The laughter subsided.

The tension of the blindfold loosened and disappeared. Once the fabric had been removed, it took a few moments for her eyes to adjust to the room. It was a man's study but not her uncle's.

Adele twisted in her chair to look at the person who removed the blindfold. She gasped.

Owen leaned against the bookcase, a cigar tucked between his satisfied smirking lips. His pressed suit and smoothed hair lent him a polished air. The glint in his eyes betrayed his enjoyment.

"Oh, my sweet, innocent cousin," he said between puffs. "Well, you are not so innocent anymore, are you?" He pushed away from the bookcase, eyeing her with the type of interest a predator shows its prey just before it attacks.

"How could you do this, Owen?" Adele jerked at her bonds hoping they would give.

"It would have been so much simpler had you remained dead, my dear." Owen sat across from her. He tisked. "How you managed to survive the fire is beyond me."

Adele gasped. "You set the fire? But why?" Angry tears pricked at her eyes.

"Does it matter?" he asked. The charming man of leisure disappeared. A man of calculated hatred sat before her.

"You cannot be the same man," she said in denial. Her cousin had always been a sweet, charming man willing to do what he could for her and her family.

Cold eyes stared back at her. "Seems I have a great talent for the stage." He took another puff of his cigar. "What I really wanted, I learned to take, sweet Adele."

The truth seemed like a nightmarish lie. Owen, it seemed, betrayed everyone who knew him with his duplicitous nature. Almost as though he had two sides to himself, a Jekyll and a Hyde. The parallel to one of her favorite books seemed almost laughable. Yet, here he stood, the evil personality incased in a once angelic man.

"Release me," she said, her voice softening. "Release me, and I will leave. I will disappear. I swear to you." A heavy ache settled in her chest.

"You will disappear, my dear, of that I can attest." He leaned forward. "But not before I use you for my own purpose."

"What do you intend to do?" she asked, fear gripping her. "They will come looking for me. Christopher will find me."

A hollow laugh filled the space between them. He stubbed out his cigar as the laugher subsided. "I certainly hope so. I cannot end this game without him."

Realization speared her heart with dread. "Please, it does not have to end this way."

"Alas, my dear, it does." Owen rose to his feet and shoved his hands in his pockets. "Dorrington will answer my questions, and then the lovers will find themselves the victims of an unfortunate fate." A wicked grin curled his lips turning a once handsome visage into a twisted mask of cruelty.

"Owen, I beg of you..." Adele pleaded. "I do not know what evil has warped your soul, but it is not too late to change your mind."

He shook his head and arched his brow. "Why would I when I am so close to obtaining my heart's desire?"

"There must be another way," she said with desperation lacing every word.

"You know," he said, running his hand over his jaw. "I should have known he was hiding you right under my nose." His gaze narrowed on her. "Did you enjoy playing the dutiful servant?" Owen shook his head.

"Please." Her heart constricted.

"Such a waste." He brushed his finger along her jaw. "Now listen, my sweet. When Dorrington arrives, I need you to remain silent."

She glared at him.

"If you refuse to obey, then I will be sure another fire finishes what the first one failed to do." Owen held her gaze for emphasis. "Your *friends* will not survive this time. I can assure you of that."

Anger soaked words soured on her tongue. She wanted nothing more than to lash out at him, but deep in her heart, she knew he would laugh them off. The serious tone laced his threat with menace. His stern warning worked. She nodded her understanding.

If she could save her friends, that would count for something.

The pounding on the front door interrupted their conversation.

"Remember what I said," Owen warned before tugging the gag back into place.

She resisted the urge to bite him.

"Silence," he reminded her before exiting the room.

Adele mumbled a quick prayer. If only Christopher could read her mind at that moment. She prayed harder.

Christopher beat his fist against the door harder. *Damn those servants! Where in the devil could they possibly be?* He braced himself to knock even louder when the door swung open.

"About damned time!" Christopher snarled.

Owen stood in the doorway of his home, catching him by surprise. "Well, old chap, this is a fine day for a visit. What brings you round so early?"

Christopher noted the crisp suit and the absence of servants. "Are you just now returning home?"

Owen shrugged and stepped aside allowing him entry into the narrow corridor. "You know how I am."

"Have you spoken to your father since yesterday?" Christopher asked. Agitation clawed at him. He needed answers damn it. He had neither the time nor inclination to play Owen's games. "Adele is missing."

Owen straightened and closed the door. "How can she be missing? Have you misplaced her?" he teased.

"Damn it! There is little time. She is gone, rest assured of that." Christopher jerked off his coat. "I believe your father had something to do with it."

"I see," Owen mused, stroking his jaw. "How do you know she has been taken, unless she has been hiding under your roof since the beginning?" A smile crossed Owen's lips. "You have been keeping her as your own little plaything, haven't you?"

"Enough with your childish taunts, Prescott." Christopher glared at him. "Yes, she is under my roof and my protection. And just as soon as she returns to society, your father demands her reunification with her *family* and she vanishes during the night."

"You believe my father took her against her will," Owen replied with a decisive snort. "You must be mad." His friend turned and gestured toward his study. "Care for a drink? You look like you could use one."

Exhausted and irritated, Christopher followed Owen through the door into the study. "I need your help finding her. You are the only one who can help me."

"I know." Owen stopped near his desk and turned. He held a pistol aimed at Christopher's heart.

"What in the devil? What is the meaning of this?" Christopher demanded before catching a glimpse of movement out of the corner of his eye.

Adele stared at him, her eyes wide, hair mussed. She tried screaming against the gag when he saw her. Her arms jerked against the bonds holding her in the chair.

His gaze swung back to Owen. "You—" Disbelief swallowed the words on his tongue.

"Sit down," Owen instructed. He jerked the barrel toward a wingback chair positioned near the far wall opposite from where Adele sat in her corner.

"I do not understand." Christopher grappled with the revelation. The betrayal stung, but it all began to make sense. Everything. How could he have been so blind? "We have been friends for years."

Owen scoffed. "We were friends, once. Then you trotted off to war like a good little soldier. Came home to a tidy inheritance and a title." His words were laced with spite and disgust. "You disappeared into your scientific world and never even noticed I had changed."

Christopher stared at him aghast. "All of this over our friendship?"

A deep rumbling laugh bubbled up from Owen's throat. He leveled his gaze with Christopher. "Do you honestly believe this is all about you?" His expression hardened like steel. "You had it all handed to you on a silver platter, and yet you squandered it by locking yourself in your lab hiding the one thing that could have changed the world and made you wealthy beyond your wildest imaginings."

The metal. Christopher shook his head. It always came back to that damned thing. "I should have left it to disappear beneath the sands."

Owen tutted. "Come now, tell me you have not dreamed of the scientific breakthroughs your little discovery could have brought into this world?"

"That damned thing has brought me nothing but misery," Christopher spat. "I lost my hand, my brother, my friends, and damn near my life because of it. I wish I never found that cursed chunk of metal."

"But I am so very glad that you did." A satisfied grin twisted Owen's lips. "You provided the perfect cover for my little endeavor. And for that, I thank you."

Christopher shook his head. "What does it matter now, the metal is gone."

"Do you expect me to believe that?" Owen leaned against the desk. The pistol remained on Christopher.

"It is the truth, whether you believe it or not," Christopher lied. He refrained from checking the pocket where the pendant lay against his body.

"If my lovely cousin survived that fire, then that metal did too. My uncle was no fool, even if he was a self-righteous arse." Owen ignored Adele's indignant squeal muffled by the gag. "I searched that house from top to bottom before I tipped that lantern, just as I tore apart that lab. One of you hid that metal, and by God, you will tell me where it is."

Christopher stared at the man whom he had once trusted like a brother. He shook his head. "How could I have missed the twisted state of your soul?"

Owen laughed again. "It has always been twisted. You just chose to ignore the signs." He cocked his head. "Once you returned, broken and grief-stricken, you lost yourself in your science experiments. When I stole those from you, opium filled the void nicely."

Denial swirled inside of him. With the truth revealed, Christopher could see the snarled, tainted friendship for what it was. Owen controlled his every move by pretending to be his friend and gaining access to parts of his life while he shuttered himself away from everyone else. While he had been so consumed with his own past and his own grief, Owen positioned himself to benefit from every avenue.

Bile bit the back of his throat. Disgust and anger raged through him. Christopher glanced at Adele. Innocent Adele who suffered just as he had at the hands of Owen's duplicity.

When he returned his gaze to Owen, he struggled to maintain his composure. There was not a single shred of regret or remorse in Owen's expression. In fact, one could say he seemed quite pleased with himself.

Owen cocked the gun. "I have seen the notes in your study. I figured you hid the metal with them." He glanced at Adele. "But I never anticipated finding *her* roaming your study in the middle of the night, wearing your robe." A lecherous grin stole across his face. "She hid it when she saw me. I am sure of that."

Christopher could sit silent no longer. He rose to his feet. "Enough!" He took a step toward Owen.

He lifted the gun level with Christopher's face. "Tell me where it is!"

"If you are going to shoot me, then do it." Christopher stepped closer.

The gun shook in Owen's hand. His brow furrowed. "I will shoot you, damn it."

Christopher raised his hands and removed his gloves. His metal hand glinted in the morning light. "Then do it already. Pull the trigger for it dies with me."

Adele screamed against the gag, thrashing against her bonds.

Owen's attention focused on her for a split second. It proved to be all the distraction Christopher needed. The madness needed to end.

He lunged at Owen and a gunshot rent the air.

Chapter Twenty

Adele's heart raced as Owen and Christopher argued. She had no choice but to listen in mute horror while the scene unfolded. But when Christopher lunged at Owen, fear seized her.

The gunshot echoed through the study.

Adele flinched at the sound, pressing her eyes closed. When she opened them, she saw Christopher and Owen wrestling on the floor. Smoke from the pistol enveloped them.

Owen struggled to gain the upper hand when Christopher knocked the pistol from his grip. It clattered across the floor, landing under the desk.

The two men scuffled, ripping at each other's throats, tearing fabric in an effort to overturn the other. Christopher landed a solid punch in Owen's side. But her cousin retaliated with a few well-placed hits of his own.

Grunting, they tussled throwing punches.

Owen caught Christopher's face with a wide swing. Christopher threw himself into Owen, knocking both men into the desk with a loud clatter.

Ink and papers flew to the floor. Owen grasped for his letter opener.

Christopher deflected the impromptu weapon with his metal hand. He twisted it from Owen's grip and tossed it away.

It became clear to Adele that Christopher had no wish to kill Owen, only incapacitate him. However, the ferocity in her cousin made it clear he intended to end it all, including the life of the man she loved.

Her heart twisted at her helplessness and the scene before her. She longed to help somehow, and yet, her situation left aid an impossibility. Instead, she watched, praying fervently.

As the fight raged on, the two men tired. Christopher knocked Owen to the floor with a stiff hook from his metal hand.

"It is not my wish to kill you," Christopher shouted as he stumbled back. Exhaustion made him sway. Blood trickled from a cut on his lip and the flesh around his eye darkened with a bruise.

Owen stumbled to his feet, resting his hand on his knee. "That is where we differ." As he stood, he reached into his pocket, removing a small derringer containing a single shot.

Adele gasped.

"Tell me where it is," he said, turning the pistol toward Adele.

Her breath caught in her throat. Staring down the barrel of a gun, Adele realized Owen would sacrifice her without hesitation.

Christopher held up his hands in surrender. "I have it." He stepped between the pistol and Adele.

She could no longer see her cousin or the gun, only the strong broad back of the man she loved.

"Let her go and I will give you what you want," Christopher relented, exhaustion evident in his voice. He reached into his pocket and extended his arm out.

Although Adele could not see what was in his hand, she knew it had to be the pendant. Her neck felt bare without it. She must have lost it in the struggle in Christopher's study. Tears pricked her eyes.

Do not trust him, she wanted to scream. Adele shouted, her words garbled by the fabric stuffed in her mouth. In her mind, she called out his name. *Christopher!*

She leaned to the side enough to see Owen reach his hand out to take the pendant. It dangled between them.

"This?" He laughed. "Clever old bastard hid it in plain sight."

When he took the pendant, Christopher caught him by the wrists, both disabling the gun and holding Owen still. Shifting his weight, he pinned him to the bookshelf, knocking the leather-bound volumes to the floor. Christopher pressed his right hand to Owen's temple.

Adele stared at the scene in agony.

A look of shock overwhelmed her cousin's expression. His agonizing scream echoed through the room. Owen dropped to his knees.

Adele wanted to cover her ears. The sound pierced her soul. After a few moments, Christopher released Owen, who fell unconscious to the floor with a thud.

Christopher picked up the pendant and tucked it in his pocket before turning to her. He rushed to her side and removed the gag before untying her.

She collapsed in his arms. "Is he dead?" she whispered against his neck. His warm, familiar scent brought her comfort against the horrors brewing in her mind.

"No," Christopher replied. "Come."

They stepped around Owen and exited the study. He held her tight while he led her toward the door. They stumbled from the house to find Andrew leading a bevy of constables up the street.

She sighed with relief.

"Get into the carriage," Christopher said, his voice low.

Adele obeyed without hesitation. She wished for nothing more than to escape the nightmare.

"Take her home, now," Christopher instructed Andrew when he approached.

Andrew nodded and glanced up at her. She smiled, and he exhaled with relief.

"I shall be home soon." Christopher kissed her hand and placed the pendant in her palm.

He closed the door and the carriage rolled into motion. She glanced out the window to see him leading the bobbies up the stairs into Owen's townhome.

Adele collapsed against the seat and wrapped her arms around herself. Tears fell uninhibited and the sobs bubbled to the surface. Her heart broke at the knowledge of her cousin, her own flesh and blood, being responsible for such horrible actions.

When the carriage stopped, Andrew helped her down and led her up the stairs to the house.

Jameson swung the door open before they reached the top step. He rushed to her side and took her arm. "I have her, Andrew, you can tend to the carriage."

Andrew gave a stiff nod and retreated.

With his arm around her, Jameson led her into the house where Elizabeth and Margaret waited. They bustled around her, fetching her fresh clothing and drawing a hot bath.

As the women took care of her, Adele's mind faded into a bleak nothingness. Numb and exhausted, she let them aid her. Fortunately, they did not press her for information.

When at last she lay soaking in a hot tub of rose scented water, Adele let the tears fall.

Christopher sat in Owen's study staring at the bookshelf lining the far wall. The volumes blended into a haze. He could only lose himself in his own thoughts.

After the bobbies escorted Owen, solemn and irate, from his townhome, Christopher remained, waiting for Longmont to arrive. He knew the fluttering of gossip would reach him. He sent a note to Lord Longmont to meet him at his son's home, post haste.

Regret filled him. How could he have been so blind to his closest companion's obvious faults?

Their scuffle left the study in chaos. Papers littered the floor, and the items that occupied the desk lay scattered around the room. Even the chair he chose had to be turned upright before he could sit. Christopher's gaze fell on the discarded bonds that held Adele captive.

Bile rose in the back of his throat.

Christopher invaded Owen's mind long enough to ascertain his motive. When he saw the reality of Owen's dark thoughts, what deprived actions he convinced himself to pursue, rage consumed Christopher. He could not allow another living thing to come to harm, not if he could stop it.

Owen would never end his quest for power, money, and status. Owen's greed blackened not only his soul, but his mind as well.

He exhaled and sprang to his feet with agitation. His own actions shocked him. His abilities sharpened since Adele's mistaken guidance introduced a way for Christopher to control it. He hesitated before searching Owen's mind, uncertain he wished to see beyond the crafted façade Owen flaunted most of his life.

Duplicity laced the memories Christopher found buried in Owen's mind. The man he had once called his friend, and a dark doppelganger who wished for that which was owed him. In an instant, Christopher glimpsed both Owen's past and his intentions.

Owen wanted them both dead, even if he had to sully his own hands in the process. He tried other methods before, but they ended fruitless.

Christopher had been able to stop Owen long enough to gain the upper hand. He twisted and warped his mind, causing unimaginable pain. While Owen screamed in agony, Christopher was able to locate the heart of Owen's consciousness and incapacitate his opponent.

It devastated him. Christopher leaned against the window frame and closed his eyes.

If I had not acted, Adele — and I — would have died. The thoughts did little to console him. The sting of betrayal and loss mixed with anger. Christopher struggled against the darkness churning in his soul.

"Dorrington, what the hell is going on?" Longmont's

voice shattered the silence.

Christopher glanced up to see Longmont standing in the doorway.

He surveyed the room with a narrow gaze, bringing it to rest on the lone occupant.

"Your son kidnapped Miss Prescott," Christopher began. He retold the story without embellishment from start to finish.

The expression on Longmont's face darkened with the deep furrow of his brows and the stern line of his lips as they pressed together.

"Owen has been arrested and taken to Scotland Yard."

When Christopher finished, Longmont nodded but remained silent. A few moments passed before either of them spoke.

"How fares my niece?" Longmont asked.

"She is safe for the moment. I saw no physical injuries that cause me concern. However, this entire ordeal will leave a barrage of traumatic scars on her mind, not to mention her heart." Christopher cleared his throat. "Owen killed her family."

"Damn that boy!" Longmont shouted. "My apologies," he said in a more controlled manner. "Had I been more aware of my son's activities and his predilections, perhaps I could have stopped him."

"Whatever drove Owen to this had been festering for a long time." Christopher collected an errant paper from the floor. "I doubt any of us could have redirected him."

Longmont shook his head. "As his father, he is my responsibility. I failed him. I failed my brother and his family." He held Christopher's gaze. "I failed you, Dorrington."

"How did you fail me?" Christopher asked, surprised by the confession.

"Had I not hounded both you and Alistair, then none of this would have happened." He smoothed his thumb over the hilt of the cane. "Owen must have seen my pursuit of your metal and the implications of its value as a quest. I never imagined it would turn into his own personal obsession."

"I believe his obsession to be much darker than that," Christopher said with a grimace. "The metal was a means to an end. It gave him the perfect cover to sabotage both Alistair and myself. I believe once he removed us from the equation, he intended to sell it to the Germans under your name."

"Treason?" Longmont shook his head and slammed the end of the cane on the wooden floor. "I refuse to believe my son is capable of treason, let alone framing me for it."

"You forget," Christopher interjected. "Owen is my closest friend. I invited him into my home and trusted him with my life. I never would have thought him capable of treason. Until I heard him confess to setting the blaze that killed your brother's family." Fury raged through him.

"He vowed to kill not only me, but Adele." Christopher stepped closer to Longmont, drawing himself up against the formidable man. "I saw the dark stain on his soul. Treason is the least of his sins."

Longmont stood still as a statue, his expression carved in marble. Christopher refused to stand down. The older man sighed.

"I cannot defend him." He waved his hand. "If he is guilty of everything you say, then he will pay for his crimes."

Relief consumed the apprehension. Christopher nodded and walked toward the door.

He paused in the doorway and turned. "Adele and I will be married by the week's end. After today, I have no intention of letting her go."

"You have my blessing, not that you needed it." Longmont offered his hand.

Christopher shook it and left Longmont standing in the ruined study.

The skies darkened with the threat of an oncoming storm. Christopher turned up his collar and shoved his hands in his pockets. His feet led him home while his mind wandered.

Chapter Twenty-One

Wrapped in a warm blanket, Adele sat in the corner of the kitchen sipping a hot toddy. The whisky soothed the frantic racing of her mind. She cradled the cup in her hand. Her attention remained on Margaret and Elizabeth who bustled back and forth preparing the evening meal.

"You need a good, hearty meal," Margaret said when Adele returned to the kitchen after her much-needed bath. She fixed her a strong drink and settled her into the chair before returning to her duties.

Adele spoke not a word, nor was she required to do so should she choose it. Every one of the staff cared for her but asked no questions. They tended her just as they had after the fire, without question, without hesitation, with concern in their eyes and love in their actions.

The fear dimmed to a nagging ache in the center of her chest. She wished Christopher would return. He took quite a few hits, thanks to Owen's pugilistic talent, and would need his injuries tended. In truth, she feared for his safety more than her own.

She flinched at the memory of the pistol trained on the man she loved. Adele set the cup aside. Her stomach churned at the thought of what could have happened.

Margaret brought a small plate of shortbread and set it beside her. "Would do you a world of good to nibble on something, my dear." She wiped her hands on her apron.

Adele smiled at her concerned expression. "My thanks." She caught a glimpse of the watch hanging from Margaret's lapel. "What time is it?"

The efficient woman unhooked the watch and peered at the small face. "Nearly four," she said with a shake of her head. "I must fix the pies."

Admiration and affection filled her. She could not have asked for a more loving group of friends to call her family. Christopher had been absent for quite a while. She prayed there had not been an incident with the police. Perhaps if she sent Andrew to be sure...

Her thoughts were cut short when Jameson entered the room. Christopher appeared after him. Streaks of dried blood marred his face. The bruises darkened to a deep purple. The haunted look in his eyes disappeared when he saw her and opened his arms.

Adele's heart soared. She leapt from her seat, dropping the blanket to the floor. Before she could stop herself, Adele threw herself into his arms. He embraced her with a ferocity that echoed down to her toes. The moment lingered until a discreet cough brought both of them back to their senses.

A glance over her shoulder made her face heat. Margaret stood dabbing her eyes with a handkerchief. Elizabeth grinned, while Jameson remained stoic as ever, even though his eyes betrayed the joy he refused to show.

"On with you then," Margaret said with a loving swat of her handkerchief. "Get out of my kitchen."

Christopher took Adele by the hand and led her upstairs to his chamber.

Once inside, he collapsed in the large chair near the fireplace with a groan.

"Would you care for a bath?" Adele asked, moving toward the adjoining wash room.

"That sounds heavenly," he replied, reaching down to remove his shoes.

Adele drew the bath, adding some salts to the water. Steam rose up from the large copper tub. Hot water had never been so simple thanks to Christopher's inventions. She lowered her hand into the water, swirling the salts until they dissolved.

"Are you going to bathe me as well?" Christopher asked

from the doorway.

She turned and her breath caught in her throat. He wore only his trousers. The taunt definition of his abdomen and the strong frame of his shoulders created a tempting landscape of flesh. Adele longed to taste every inch of him.

She nodded, clearing the wicked thoughts from her mind. "I intend to examine those cuts and bruises, but first, you need to wash."

Keeping his gaze locked with hers, he unfastened his trousers and slipped them down over his hips. They fell to the floor leaving him bare. He smiled at her reaction.

Heat rose to her cheeks, but the steam could have been affecting her as well. She cleared her throat.

"Well then, in you get." She gestured to the bath before turning to shut off the water. Adele licked her lips and inhaled deeply before exhaling. She would not let him affect her, at least not until she was certain his injures were tended.

The water splashed, catching her attention. Christopher lowered himself into the bath. As he settled, he rested his hand on Adele's arm.

"Does this make you uncomfortable?" he asked with amusement.

She plucked a rag from the shelf and dipped it into the water. "Not at all," she lied.

With tender care, Adele washed his face, removing the blood. A few cuts, and more than several darkening bruises, but nothing that would not heal with time. As she worked, he studied her face. Her heart raced and her body warmed with awareness of his attention.

Anxious to ease the sexual tension rising between them, Adele broke the silence by focusing on something other than her body's reactions to him. "How is my cousin?"

Christopher sighed and closed his eyes before leaning back against the rim of the tub. "He is in prison."

Adele nodded and a weight lifted from her heart even though sadness lingered there. "Why would he do such horrible things to his own flesh and blood?" she asked.

"Only he would know the answer to what lies in the dark, twisted recesses of his mind." Christopher took her chin in his hand. He gasped at the contact and released her.

"You know the truth." She remembered his ability, even though he hid it so well. "You invaded his mind."

Christopher ran his hand over his face. "I wish to God I had never done it." He shook his head. "The things I have seen, the things I now know, I wish I could forget."

"Tell me why he killed my parents," she begged. The tears spilled from her eyes without provocation. She let them fall.

"He concocted this twisted plan. I am not sure if it would have ever worked, but Owen believed it would."

"What plan?" she asked.

Christopher dipped beneath the water. Adele knew the conversation would be painful for both of them, but she deserved to hear the truth. He resurfaced and grabbed a towel.

She backed away as he stepped from the water and dried himself. Adele worried Christopher would never tell her. The longer the silence stretched between them, the more frustrated she became.

Once he pulled his robe on, Christopher reached for her.

"Forgive me." He drew her into his arms. "He may have been my friend, but he was your cousin." Christopher led her into the bedroom and sat down in the chair near the fire. He pulled her into his lap. "Betrayal stings, but Owen's actions are unconscionable. What he did to you and your family —" He shook his head " — is truly heinous."

"Tell me," she murmured and nestled closer to him absorbing his warmth and comfort. "I must know."

Christopher sighed. "He sabotaged the lab, set the fire, and tried to steal my metal along with all the research. That much you know." With a deep breath, he continued. "He wished to sell the metal to Germany, knowing it held great scientific value with its conductive properties."

Adele gasped. "But that would be treason."

Christopher nodded. "His intention was to sell it under his father's name and lead the authorities to Lord Longmont in order to frame him for treason." He held her tight. "By removing your family and his father from the equation, Owen would inherit the title and both fortunes."

"So, my uncle had no part of his plot." Adele curled into his warmth.

"None at all." Christopher smoothed his hand over her hip. "In fact, he seemed quite shocked about the whole thing."

"What of Musgrave?" she asked, remembering the man who once been a friend of her family.

"Owen killed him when he refused to tell him anything about the metal." Sadness creased Christopher's brow. "The cufflink was Owen's. Damn if I didn't notice it before!" He scowled harder.

She longed to soothe it away, so she kissed his forehead. "There was nothing to be done, my love." Emotion constricted her throat. "He has chosen his path, and now he must accept the consequences of his actions."

Christopher's hands grazed over her hip and along her side until he turned her to face him. She admired his bewitching eyes and the tilt of his mouth. The injuries did nothing to distract from his handsome features. In fact, they lent him a rugged, roguish charm.

She caressed his face.

He sucked in a sharp breath. "I have very little strength remaining with which to fend off your thoughts, darling."

Adele smiled and brushed her fingertips across his lips. She withdrew the necklace from the pocket hidden in the folds of her skirt. "I cannot wear this," she exclaimed, holding the pendant by the broken chain.

"Damn," he mumbled. "Wait a moment." Christopher lifted her to her feet and disappeared into the next room. When he returned, a length of ribbon dangled from his fingers. Within moments he threaded the pendant with the ribbon and motioned for her to turn.

She swept her hair to the side. Without effort, he placed the ribbon around her neck. The pendant hung between her breasts where it hummed with warm satisfaction.

"Shall we see if it works?" she teased him by leaning closer.

Christopher's lips crashed down onto hers, betraying his hunger. She moaned and kissed him back with all the passion she contained inside.

Adele gasped, breathless as he pulled her down with him into the chair once more.

"What am I thinking?" She murmured the question against his mouth between kisses.

Christopher pulled back and arched his brow. His lips curled into an amused smirk. "My love, if it is anything like what you were thinking before I put the pendant on you, then you would be scandalized if I voiced them aloud."

She bit her lip with embarrassment. "Yes, well, what am I thinking right now?"

"I love you," he whispered, bringing his mouth to her jaw and trailing it over her neck.

"Close enough." Adele gave in to the sensations and surrendered to the knowledge that he loved her. She had found her family and her place in the world at last. And so they began a new adventure together.

The End

Other Books By Kirsten S. Blacketer

CRAVING 1985 SERIES

When I Found You
Can't Fight This Feeling
She Gives Love a Bad Name
Owner of a Lonely Heart
Just What I Needed

HISTORICAL

An Irresistible Shadow
A Shadow's Kiss
Mississippi Moonshine
Deceiving the Earl
Jewel of Winter
At Winter's Demand
Under Winter's Control
Seducing Winter's Gentleman
Stealing the Widow's Heart
Seduction on the Alpine Express
Temptation on the Alpine Express

CONTEMPORARY

A Lockdown Love Affair
A Holiday Love Affair
Mistletoe and Mistakes
Confessions of a Fangirl
Confessions of a Gamer Girl
Confessions of a Glamour Girl
The Flight Before Christmas

FANTASY/FAIRYTALE

Curse of the Huntsman's Jewel
The Huntsman's Revenge

PIRATES AND PERSUASION

Queen Takes Hook

About the Author
Kirsten S. Blacketer

Kirsten S. Blacketer is a multi-published indie author of both historical and contemporary romance. When she's not writing, she homeschools her two children and enjoys time with her family. In those moments of freedom, she devours romance novels while sipping a glass of wine. Age has only shown her that writing villains can be just as fun as heroes. Her next life goals are to write a New York Times Bestseller and one day have Adam Driver play a starring role in a film version of one of her books. A girl can dream, right?

Read more at **http://kirstensblacketer.com.**

ALSO WRITES AS JEN BRADLEE